Spyrius Technology:
Oz Imagined

Published 2015 by John Connor - Spyrius Technology

Copyright © 2015 by John Connor

ISBN 978-0-9965312-0-7

Library of Congress Control Number: 2015910151

3nd Printing

www.spyriustechnology.com

Cover illustration and design by Holly Heisey, http://hollyheisey.com

For my Godson Lucas

Contents

Chapter 1

The man standing at the door to our apartment was from Spyrius Technology. This was very odd.

Spyrius (pronounced spear•e•us) Technology is the newest and 'coolest' computer company out there. In just three years they have gone from nothing to a multi something dollar business making the most cutting-edge computers and operating systems available. Their computers are sleek, new and futuristic with technologies that none of the other big computer giants have, or at least have that work well. Their computers offer things like 3D screens that don't require glasses, virtual touch screens that recognize hand and finger movements, voice technology that processes intent as well as direct commands, latest biometric security and a host of other features. Of course you pay for this, and their machines are nothing if not expensive. I would know. I somehow managed to talk my parents into getting one of their latest and greatest laptops for my sophomore year at college, which I'm just starting.

The other main thing about Spyrius is their notorious secrecy in all aspects of their company. From their new headquarters in a remote place called Moses Lake in the state of Washington, encircled with barbed wire and watchtowers more reminiscent of a prison than a high-tech company, to the rumored agreements that all employees must sign, stating that they will not discuss any aspect of the company outside of campus for any reason. Not that this has had any impact in Spyrius's ability to sign the latest and greatest talent to the company. The idea that one can work on the newest and most interesting technologies from direct brain interfaces to covert military contracts (at least that is what is rumored), entices many, including myself. As a computer science major fascinated by cutting-edge technology, the idea of working for someone as cool and secretive, that supposedly pays really well too, would be a dream come true.

So it was for this reason that I had a mix of excitement and wonderment as to why this man, dressed in the very obvious bright red shirt of Spyrius, was standing at the door of the average, though newly built, off-campus apartment that I shared with my two roommates. The man was big and imposing, with the business-like look of a Secret Service agent. Not unfriendly, mind you, but probably not the type who would accept an invitation for a round of drinks at a bar after.

"Joshua Amandil?"

"Yes, that's me."

"My name is Phil and I am a representative from Spyrius Technologies. May I come in?"

I let the man in. He talked in the same matter-of-fact way that he appeared, and I noticed that he did not volunteer a last name. Regardless I brought him into the main room of our modest-sized abode. Our place is in a brand new building, just built to house the ever increasing student base at the Virginia Polytechnic Institute, or Virginia Tech for short, where I go to. The apartment has one great room that encompasses the kitchen, dining and living area as well as two bedrooms and two full baths. Spartan and basic, with clean simple lines, it has all the necessities for college students. I invited the man to sit down at our kitchen table. He stayed standing.

"Larry, Sylvia, this is Phil from Spyrius Technologies, Phil, these are my roommates Larry and Sylvia."

Indeed, Larry Trumbald and Sylvia Hitchcock were my two roommates. They said hi, the man said nothing.

"I will get right down to business." The man from Spyrius stated. "There seems to have been a mistake when you were given this apartment. You were actually supposed to get one on the third floor, but management accidently gave you the wrong place."

On the face of it this seemed to be a very odd statement, but it did make a modicum of sense. From the time the three of us picked up the keys and moved in yesterday, we all wondered how we ended up so lucky as to land what seemed like the best unit in the building. The floor plans of all the units were essentially the same mix of sparsely decorated one and two bedroom flats, but our unit was on the sixth floor, which was the highest, with a beautiful view on the side that overlooked campus, as opposed to the other side that overlooked a road. For a group of sophomores, in a building with plenty of upperclassmen, graduate students, and even a few professors, supposedly, it just seemed too good to be true. But when we asked we were told by the manager that this was our room, so we went with it.

Larry, Sylvia and I looked at each other, trying to figure out how to respond. When none of us did the man went on.

"I understand how this would be an inconvenience to you since you already moved your belongings in, and I do understand that this room does have a nice view…" as if he was reading my mind, "but the room on the third floor still faces the campus and should be satisfactory."

Still neither of us said anything, not quite sure how to respond, or for that matter why a man from a technology company was the one asking us to relocate.

"And to help out with your inconvenience due to this misunderstanding, Spyrius would like to offer the three of you this token as an apology."

The man reached into a jacket pocket and pulled out a thick envelope. He opened it up and pulled out a handful of cash. Not just random cash, but five half-inch thick bundles of twenty dollar bills wrapped with the same seals that banks use to wrap their cash.

"I hope $10,000 cash will help ease your transition."

His hand extended the cash in my direction as both Larry and Sylvia, suddenly jolted into reality, chimed in together, "Ten thousand dollars!"

What I did next is still a mystery to me. Something deep inside my unconscious was moving much faster in interpreting this situation than was my conscious mind, and what came forth from my mouth was not what my conscious self was thinking at all.

"Thanks, but no thanks. We like this apartment, it was the apartment that was given to us and we will keep it. We appreciate your offer but good day."

I have no idea who was more surprised at what I said: Larry and Sylvia, the man, or me. Larry and Sylvia both shot looks at me that seemed to imply that we should not be so hasty to say no. However my conscious mind was slowing starting to catch up to what my unconscious blurted out so quickly, and I was becoming more assured that there was a good reason for not taking what this man was offering us. Either way, the man, Phil, was clearly not expecting an 18 year old college student to not only decline his offer, but tell him to leave. He seemed unsure of his next move, which probably was foreign to a man who was most likely trained to always be in control of a situation. He quickly gathered himself and made one last insistent offer.

"I think it would be a mistake for you not to take my offer."

He said this firmly, and it sounded vaguely like a threat. I think he realized that and checked his tone.

"Are you sure you do not want to take this? It might not be available again."

This he said far less threatening, and it made me realize that he was not going to push the situation. Regardless of whether he was here by company order, I was pretty sure he had no legal standing and that if I relented he would leave. At least for the time being.

"No, I am sure. We are not interested. Thank you for the offer, but would you please leave."

"Wait a second…"

That was Sylvia chiming in, as I am sure she wanted to debate this a bit more. Ten thousand dollars is a lot of money to three college students. But I cut her off before she got another word out.

"The lease is in my name, and we are staying in this apartment."

I looked straight at Sylvia, and I think she was very startled by my firmness on this. Fortunately I think she understood that I had my reasons and knew me well enough to trust me. Or maybe she was just curious as to why I would firmly turn down the offer. Regardless, even though getting this place together was Larry's idea, the lease was indeed in my name as my parents were the only one of the three sets of parents willing to co-sign for it. So in a way I did have the final say.

"I am sorry you feel this way. I will leave, but enjoy your only two nights in this apartment. On Monday morning you will be legally removed from this apartment and placed into the other, but without your relocation fee."

He put extra emphasis on the last part, put the money back into his jacket pocket, turned and left, closing the door behind him.

At this point I dropped into one of the kitchen chairs shaking. I was suddenly overwhelmed, not quite believing that I had just stood up to an agent from Spyrius Technology and called his bluff. After all, I was a computer geek who has never been in a truly intimidating situation in his life. I didn't know how to handle those kinds of situations, yet somehow I did. It was Larry who actually broke the tension.

"That would make three nights. Doesn't he know we stayed here last night too?"

Larry and I were roommates by happenstance during our freshman year when we were matched together in our dorm room. Slightly overweight, but generally in good shape Larry's laid-back with an easygoing personality that goes well with being a poli-sci major. Never one to be in the foreground, one could easily see him as part of a think tank or a politician's A-team. He would be the one to mull over the data, reflect, take his time and then propose a sound, if not groundbreaking, solution. Larry's the type of person everyone likes and gets along with, but yet isn't quite memorable.

This is very much in contrast to my personality. I am a type-A, hyper-dorky computer geek with the thin, high metabolism, glasses-wearing build you would expect. To add to my stereotypical appearance, I started grade school early, so I was always one of the youngest in my class, and just have a youthful appearance in general. I tend to be more forward, more opinionated and more annoying at times, though not nearly as much as my best friend Kyle, who will enter the story shortly. Basically Larry and I do not have much in common and, while we are friends, it's not like either thinks this will be one of those lifelong friendships that lasts past college. One of those where you say, 'let's stay in touch', but then slowly lose track of each other over time until you realize you haven't talked in years and what's the point anymore. But I think it's because of those differences and our not too close relationship that we get along so well as roommates. We will eat dinner together, watch TV together and walk to class together when our paths cross all with friendly banter between us, yet still manage to keep a certain emotional distance.

Sylvia is the wild card. She is Larry's girlfriend and has been since they first met at the very beginning of our collective freshman year. Tall, thin and mostly attractive with a bit of mystery, Sylvia reminds you of a secret agent who seems friendly, but whose ultimate motives you are never quite sure of. It's like there is some part of her personality she does not want to know about, and makes sure it stays that way. Either way, Larry and Sylvia's relationship grew pretty strong throughout last year and continued strong through the summer even though Sylvia lives near Roanoke, while Larry lives about three hours away in the suburbs of Richmond. I think Sylvia likes the fact that she basically runs the relationship even though Larry thinks he does, or at least would tell you it's on equal terms if you asked.

I like Sylvia, mystery and all, and get along with her great. She seems to see me, and the aforementioned Kyle, as bratty little brothers that annoy her at times but that she still loves, thinks are sweet, and wants to mother a little. I give credit to both Larry and Sylvia for never making me feel uncomfortable when Larry and I shared a room. They were never overly affectionate in front of me (not that either are really outwardly affectionate people to begin with) and never tried to get rid of me for private time. It was for that reason that I went along with their idea of sharing an apartment with them for our sophomore year. I figured if we all got along well when Larry and I were stuck in a single room together with Sylvia as a frequent guest, then having separate bedrooms would make for a harmonious household. From their point of view I knew they thought of me as a known entity that could help out with the rent. How having Sylvia around full time would affect Larry's and my relationship I did not know, but I was willing to give it a try. It also gave me the excuse I needed to not share a dorm or apartment with Kyle for reasons I will get into in a bit.

Larry nicely inquired on why I turned down ten grand, but Sylvia was a bit more forward. "Okay mister, what's going on? Just when did you suddenly grow balls? And you better have a good reason for at least not thinking about that man's offer."

I told her to hold on a second. It was only 1:00 in the afternoon, but after that little episode I needed a drink.

It was Saturday and we had pretty much just finished setting everything up from moving in. All three of us came down Friday with my parents driving me down from Northern Virginia in the family Jeep with my mattress tied to the top. Larry rented a U-Haul and drove himself, along with his couch, kitchen table and a few other pieces of furniture from Richmond. He stopped by Sylvia's in Roanoke to get the bed the two of them would share and then Sylvia, the only one of us with a car, followed in her generic used sedan. I gulped down a small glass half full of Coke and half full of cheap vodka. It was awful, but I needed it.

"I have no idea how to answer your first two questions. But hear me out on the third. Look, we're just some dumb, anonymous college kids, and here comes a representative from one of the biggest, richest and most secretive companies in the world just showing up at our door offering us *ten thousand dollars*. Now they didn't come with the building manager, or the police. They just tried to get us out of here with a quick bribe. Why?"

"How should I know?" Sylvia responded.

"Well I don't know either, but whatever the reason is I am betting that it's worth more than ten thousand dollars. A lot more."

Sylvia shot back, "I am pretty certain that they will be back with some sort of legal document evicting us on Monday morning. So, you are betting ten grand that we are going to find something worth more than that in this apartment by then? Oh, and even if we find something, do you think we are just going to be able to sell it? It's not like we will own it, if there even is an 'it'."

"I know, I know. But this is Spyrius. Anyone else and I would take the money, but Spyrius? It has to be something really, really cool."

Forgot to mention earlier, but Spyrius as a company is rich. Well supposedly, as they are a private company, no one really knows for sure... What the public does know is that they were founded and are run by one Sebastian Danbridge, only child and sole heir of the deceased billionaire oil baron Roderick Danbridge. Sebastian, better known as Lord Danbridge, which he supposedly likes to be called by, is a slightly odd recluse, almost on par with Howard Hughes, and supposedly a genius. After selling his dad's old company for a few billion dollars he plowed it all into Spyrius, gobbled up a bunch of cutting-edge startups and folded them into his company.

"Well I don't know about you," Larry chimed in, "but I don't remember seeing anything out of the ordinary other than that extra dryer outlet, and we've moved stuff into all corners of this place over the last day. So where do we begin?"

"I don't know," I said, "Maybe there's a secret room, or a loose floorboard or something. Or maybe the paint has microprocessors embedded in it, or... I don't know."

"Great," Larry responded dejectedly.

"I know I'm going to regret this," Sylvia sighed, "And it pains me to say it... But get Kyle over here."

Chapter 2

"Okay, let me get this straight. A guy from Spyrius just shows up at your door, offers you ten thousand dollars cash to switch apartments, and you tell him no and kick him out solely on the hunch that something better than ten grand is in this apartment? Awesome! Maybe my natural distrust of authority figures is finally rubbing off on you, Josh."

That's Kyle. Kyle Frost has been my best friend since we first met in a gaming club in our freshman year of high school. Kyle, like me, is a computer geek with a high metabolism who wears glasses. People sometimes think we are brothers even though he has freckles, a lighter complexion and light colored hair in comparison to my darker complexion and dark brown hair. But, whereas I am pretty normal in almost all aspects, just on the geek end of the spectrum, Kyle is not. Kyle is needy, suffers from low self-esteem and is extremely socially awkward when out of his comfort zone. Oh, and yeah, he is a genius. I don't mean just smart, like I tend to think of myself, but I mean a real genius. He scored perfect 800s on each part of the SAT's, has an almost photographic memory and has an uncanny ability to just understand complex problems of all types. So if anyone could make sense of our situation and provide insight, it would be Kyle.

"So why *do* you have an extra dryer outlet on the other side of the room?"

That was a question none of us could answer for Kyle. Our apartment had a closet-sized area where an included stacked washer/dryer combo resided. The electric dryer plugged into one of those big 240 volt dryer outlets in the closet. The odd thing was that there was an extra 240 volt outlet on a wall in the main room, next to a normal 120 volt outlet.

"Josh, you said this Spyrius guy offered you an apartment on the third floor facing the campus, right?" I nodded in the affirmative. "Sylvia, go down to the building manager's office and use your charms to find out who rented whatever currently vacant unit is on the third floor facing campus side. It's two o'clock on the Saturday everyone moves in; he will be there. And while you are going down, poke into a couple of other apartments like this one that have people moving things in and out and see if they have that extra 240 volt outlet. Pretend you are just being neighborly or something."

"Yes sir, captain," Sylvia responded with a military salute, got up, checked her hair and makeup and left.

Kyle started walking around into each room with the look of a seasoned detective observing a crime scene for the first time. He pulled down the blinds in case anyone was watching from the outside and then began to tap on walls and floors and take measurements with a borrowed tape measure. He looked into light fixtures, and behind appliances, taking everything in while Larry and I just watched. Finally, after about twenty minutes, he stopped.

"You have two intake vents, and that one makes no sense."

Before either Larry or I could ask what he meant by that Sylvia came back. We all waited for her report.

"Poked my head into three different apartments like ours. Real easy with all the people moving stuff in. By the way, there are two gay guys at the end of the hall, real friendly, and on the third floor someone has a small dog. I didn't know you could have a dog here. We need to get a dog."

"Focus on the task, Sylvia."

"Sorry Kyle."

"It's a $500 deposit for the dog and it must be under forty pounds," I interjected, which was met with a nasty look from Kyle. Sylvia continued.

"None of the other apartments have the extra outlet. There is one unit on the third floor on this side of the building that is unoccupied. I asked the super about it. I made up a story about my friend from last year, saying that's where she would be and I wanted to check in case I was wrong. Get this: he actually admitted we might have been given this apartment by mistake. He said someone came this morning to claim this apartment, 6C, under the name Eliza Weizenbaum, but that 3C, the vacant apartment, had that name on it, and 6C had ours. He said the man, so obviously not this Eliza as it was a man, was not happy, but the super said he couldn't do anything until corporate offices open Monday morning. The odd thing was that the man he described was definitely not the Phil guy who visited us, but someone else entirely."

"Did you say Eliza Weizenbaum?" shot Kyle with a look of wild abandonment. He immediately pulled out his smart phone, quickly looked something up and then exclaimed, "Just what I thought, and we just hit the jackpot!"

"What jackpot? What are you talking about?" Larry asked.

"There is something that Spyrius Technology is doing that requires this particular apartment and we have this weekend to hopefully find out why. Eliza Weizenbaum..." Kyle mulled to himself, "that's definitely something straight from the mind of Lord Danbridge."

We all asked Kyle who in the heck was Eliza Weizenbaum?

"It's not a who, it's a computer program. ELIZA was the very first pseudo-artificial intelligence program, written at M.I.T. back in the Sixties. An armchair psychologist so to speak. It was a sham actually; it basically just reflected back what you said to her, it, whatever, but it fooled a lot of people who thought it was real artificial intelligence. It was written by this guy named Weizenbaum. Spyrius is involved in a project to develop a true web-based artificial intelligence psychologist that could be used like a crisis hotline-type thing. Not that I believe in coincidences anyway, but this is no coincidence. Plus that intake vent up there makes no sense."

"Go on."

"Well, Larry, you have one on that wall that seems to make sense, but the other one just doesn't seem like it would route properly to the furnace. I just turned the heat up; I think it's on now."

"But it's not that cold." Larry said quizzically.

"That's not the point. Watch."

Kyle took a piece of paper and put it over the one intake. The paper stuck to the intake as it was being sucked in by the air. Then he took the paper over to the other, and nothing. It just fell harmlessly to the floor. "Give me a chair and a screwdriver," he said as he proceeded to unscrew the intake cover. Instead of some ductwork to transport air there was a shelf, and recessed back into the shelf was a safe. A decent-sized safe at that: probably one and a half feet square, and white so it blended in behind the white intake cover. It had both a combination lock and a key lock. This was good because I knew the key lock could probably be picked.

"Josh, you got the lock pick kit you bought at DefCon?"

"You bet, Kyle," I answered as I went into my room to find the lock pick kit that I knew was buried somewhere in my unpacked suitcase.

Lock picking is one of Kyle's many talents. Kyle's father is a semi-celebrity in the ethical hacking community, and he has been taking Kyle to the DefCon computer hacking convention in Las Vegas since he was ten years old. One of the things you can learn there is lock picking, among many other semi-nefarious things. So he learned and practiced lock picking to the point where he became an expert. I went with them two years ago and it was a blast, though Kyle's dad didn't invite me last year. He tolerates me, but I am pretty sure he thinks I am not smart enough to be friends with his kid. Of course no one is, so I am not sure what he wants. I think he blames me for Kyle going to Tech, which is probably true enough. Kyle could have easily gone to M.I.T., Carnegie Mellon or some other top-rated tech school, but I think he was too afraid to go someplace on his own without someone he knows (translation: me) around. When I was out there with him I bought a set of lock pick tools. I never really use them, as Kyle is normally around and he can run rings around me when it comes to opening locks, but I keep them around and that saved us the trouble of having to run back to Kyle's dorm room for his set.

The three of us sat silently and watched Kyle ply his trade. It wasn't easy for him. He had to stand on a chair with a couple of thick textbooks on top of that to get to the right height, so I am sure it was not the most comfortable position to try. I don't really know what Larry or Sylvia were thinking. Neither offered up any resistance to the idea of trying to pick the lock. I'm not really sure about the legality of what we were doing, but ultimately this was our apartment. I had a go for it attitude. After all, we had gone this far, why stop now? I know Kyle had no issues, as smart as he is, he has always had the do first and worry about the consequences later way of thinking. It's Larry who I thought might offer up a cautionary note, but none came. So if he was not offering resistance then it was okay with me.

The minutes ticked by, the silence only broken by the occasional, "damn it," by Kyle. Picking a lock is all feel, slowly pushing each bound pin in order until it hits its sheer line, allowing you to turn the lock ever so slightly with a tension wrench until you get the last one. All locks are not created equal though, some are much harder than others and you have to assume a fairly substantial looking safe would be on the hard side. To be honest though, I was not too worried that he would eventually crack it. Even though Kyle was only eighteen he had been practicing this trade for years and learned from experts each time at DefCon such that he was as much an expert lock pick as anyone else in the country. We have all seen Kyle open some pretty nasty-looking padlocks (as well as dorm door locks, but those take a few seconds - even I can do those). He just needed silence and total concentration.

After about twenty minutes I was ready to see if Kyle wanted a break or needed anything but then we all heard the click. Kyle didn't say a word, he just turned and faced us with a big smile of immense satisfaction on his face as he slowly opened the safe door without even looking in. I actually think some tears were welling in his eyes. He was beaming with pride. My occasional big brother instincts with Kyle kicked in (he is two weeks younger than me after all) and I told him we were proud of him and reached up to give him a pat on the back.

Sylvia, however, was having nothing of the touching moment, "Well, what the hell is in it?"

"Hmm," he considered as he looked into the safe. "There's a DVD, or Blu-Ray, or whatever," handing the disk down to me, "and something very odd…"

The last trailed off as he brought out what looked like a projector. It was a little over a foot wide, about a foot high (barely fitting in the safe) with a large lens in the front and a power switch on top. The odd thing was that it looked homemade. Not homemade like the average person would make, but very well-made like something a craftsman would do. It was all metal and definitely not something you could buy in a store. And it was heavy - very heavy. Larry had to get another chair and help Kyle get it out of the safe and all four of us helped to get it down onto the kitchen table.

Out from the back were two hard wired cords. One was about two feet long and terminated in a regular USB plug. The other was the power cord, but instead of the normal cord and plug it was a thick cord that terminated with a 240 volt dryer plug.

"I think we just figured out why there is an extra dryer plug in this room," I said.

We examined it from all angles. I was thinking that there must be a big transformer in that thing, and whatever kind of projector it was, it needed a lot of juice to run it. Larry, the methodical one, took over as group leader for the moment and went over the situation logically.

"Alright, let's take stock of what we have here:

> First, I think we can safely assume this is some prototype something from Spyrius Technology but we have no idea what it does or if it is even safe. So before we go plugging it in I think we need to learn a bit more.

> Second, we have a disk of some sort. I say we start there and see what is on it, whether it is a program or a movie or whatever, as it might shed some light on this monstrosity. Josh, you have a Spyrius computer - let's try to read the disk and see what might be on it."

"Oh Larry, your no fun."

That came from Kyle, who probably would have just plugged the thing into the wall, but Larry was defiantly right. We needed to learn as much as we could about this machine and the disk that came with it was probably the best start. I did have one idea.

"Spyrius does have holographic projection technology," I stated. "I saw a video on it not too long ago, but this projector seems way too big and heavy for that. I think? Maybe? Let's see."

I put the disk into my Spyrius laptop and opened up a graphic file manager. There were several folders on the Blu-Ray disk, but I realized that we needed to be more methodical before going any further.

"I probably should make a backup of the whole disk first. I'll go ahead and create an image file and burn it to a backup disk. This way we can keep the backup just in case and we can put the original back into the safe."

Everyone nodded in agreement and I started the process. While that was going on in the background we explored the file structure in the file manager. The main disk had just three folders and nothing else. They were:

- *Oz*
- *Oz Creation*
- *Oz Data*

"Well the only Oz I know is the Wizard of Oz," Sylvia pointed out.

"I think there was a TV series called *Oz*," Larry said.

No one else had a response so I continued examining the folder structure. Under the *Oz* folder was an executable program simply entitled 'Install' and a bunch of related folders that looked to be data files and linked libraries that went with the program. It was obvious that this was a program meant to be installed on the computer. Just by looking at the related files, both Kyle, who also had a Spyrius laptop, though a year older than mine, and I could determine that this was a native Spyrius application meant to run on a Spyrius machine.

The *Oz Creation* folder was similar, with an 'Install' program, related files, and a native application. The *Oz Data* file was empty save for two zero byte files whose names were 'ALWAYS SYNC AND DOWNLOAD LATEST DATA FILES' and 'LOCK YOUR AREA

BEFORE MODIFYING'. Obviously these files weren't files at all, but were just being used to convey a warning.

What was missing was any sort of documentation files that might give us some clue to whatever these programs were for. Kyle offered the most logical explanation after I pointed this out.

"I think we can assume these programs probably work with the projector, and that this is some internal Spyrius project. There probably is no documentation because whoever would be working with this is probably already well-versed and fully trained in using whatever the heck it is."

"Well obviously we need to install these programs," I said, mostly to Kyle. We were in Kyle's and my world now; Larry and Sylvia were just along for the ride. "Which program should I install first?"

"I'm thinking the program in the *Oz* folder has to be the main program. I would actually install the one in the *Oz Creation* folder first and see what that is."

"I concur."

The image had been created at this point. I got a blank Blu-Ray disk from my room and started creating a backup. That would take a few minutes and we all realized we were pretty hungry. My mom went to the local supermarket with me before her and my dad left for home, so the fridge was stocked pretty well with food. We all made some sandwiches from the cold cuts she bought. As we ate, Sylvia surprised Kyle and me with a fairly astute technical observation.

"You should probably turn off the Wi-Fi before you install any of these programs, just in case it wants to phone back home."

"Good idea," I said. "If nothing else at least we might be able to know if it's trying to connect to the Internet for anything."

Kyle just looked at Sylvia in surprise.

"What?" exclaimed Sylvia. "It's not like Larry and I have no computer skills. You know I did take a basic programming course in high school."

Sylvia was majoring in psychology, but she actually wanted to be a lawyer. While most lawyers pursue some sort of business degree it seems psychology is not a totally uncommon undergrad degree for lawyers. After all if you are trying to sway a judge or jury, psychology comes in handy. I took the basic Psychology 101 course last year and enjoyed it quite a bit. Sylvia and I would compare notes about the different neuroses of everyone we knew, including Larry but especially Kyle.

You see, Kyle's family situation is not one that provides the most nurturing of conditions. I really didn't pay attention to it until I took Psychology and was enlightened to the full dysfunction of Kyle's home life. His parents are both extremely smart and very career-oriented. As stated, his dad is a semi-celebrity ethical hacker who travels the world over consulting with major corporations, giving speeches and writing articles and books. Kyle idolizes his dad, but the only time he gets to spend with him is at some hacking event, like DefCon. I don't think his dad would know how to take Kyle fishing if the fish swam into their bathtub and turned over dead.

Kyle's mom is not much better. A D.C. lawyer lobbying for some non-profit digital rights group, she is neck deep in her work as well. Add to that the fact that Kyle is an only child with no sibling to interact with and you end up with a very lonely kid. There was one time in high school when Kyle got a drug pipe and left it on the floor of his room. Nope, he didn't do drugs at all, he just wanted to get attention from his parents even if it was negative attention. They didn't notice, or if they did, they did not care.

So Kyle provided plenty for Sylvia and me to discuss what we learned in class and how it applied to him. Needless to say we have never told Kyle about this hobby of ours.

Lunch done and disk burned I clicked on the *Oz Creation* 'Install.' It did not take too long for the install to finish, and with some trepidation I went ahead and clicked on the newly created *Oz Creator* icon. We were all huddled around the laptop, not quite sure what to expect, but expecting something magical none the less. What appeared was pretty anti-climactic. A terminal window opened stating:

Cannot sync to Oz

"So much for my bright idea of turning off the Wi-Fi."

"Good idea Sylvia," I said, "but nowadays everything requires network connectivity."

Kyle came up with an idea though. "Josh, run the network analyzer, capture the traffic and then re-run the program. We should be able to see where it is trying to go to and look it up on *WhoIs*."

Larry and Sylvia had no idea what Kyle was talking about, but I thought it was a great idea. I explained it to them.

"The program is trying to connect to somewhere though an IP address. It's no different than connecting to a website with a web browser. In that case the website you are connecting to has a specific IP address behind it. In this case the program is connecting to somewhere using an IP address. Kind of like E.T. phoning home. We can watch to see where it is trying to connect to and then look up that address using the *WhoIs* database, akin to looking up a phone number in a phone book, and then we may get some clues as to where the program is trying to go."

"Nobody uses phone books anymore," Sylvia noted.

"Install and click on *Oz*," pleaded Kyle, "it will probably give us the same error; we can test that one too."

Before Larry or Sylvia could object, I installed *Oz*. It gave me a single icon simply called *Oz*, and I clicked on it. Not only did I get the same '*Cannot sync to Oz*' error, but I also received a '*Cannot connect to projector*' error message. At least we now were almost certain that the oversized projector was meant to interface with this program.

I fired up SpyriusShark, a network analysis program, or sniffer, which would allow us to track down the IP address these programs were trying to connect to. It's just the Spyrius native application clone of WireShark, a network sniffer for Windows and Unix. Turning it on so it would capture all attempted traffic, we ran both the *Oz Creator* and *Oz* programs, noting the IP address for each. We got 203.0.113.8 for *Oz Creator*, 203.0.113.16 for *Oz*. Using Larry's computer we put those into the *WhoIs* database and the following was the same output for both:

Whois	*IP 203.0.113.8 (16)*
NetRange:	*203.0.113.0 - 203.0.113.255*
Organization:	*Spyrius Technology*
Address:	*One Spyrius Way*
City:	*Moses Lake*
StateProv:	*WA*
PostalCode:	*98837*
Country:	*US*
OrgTechEmail:	*info@spyriustechnology.com*

"Well we can't say they are trying to hide anything," noted Sylvia.

"I think," Kyle mused, "that this being an internal project, the accessibility of this information doesn't really matter. Spyrius has lots of IP address ranges. Plus, you noticed it was connecting via HTTPS, which is encrypted, so no one can actually examine the data while in transit."

I pointed out that at least we knew for sure know that this was something from Spyrius Technology.

"So what now?" posed Larry.

I think all of us knew that in order to even have a chance to see whatever this program and projector might do we would be exposing ourselves to Spyrius. They would most likely know instantly that we were connecting with this 'thing' that we were obviously not supposed have. The ramifications of that were totally unknown, as was what would happen if we even fired up the projector and program. I pointed this out to all to ensure that each of us understood the risks and could make an educated decision on proceeding. Kyle may have been well-educated, but he spoke more with the enthusiasm of a five-year-old opening his birthday presents.

"Larry, Sylvia, Josh: any of you can back out if you want to. I can even take this somewhere else if you don't want to do it here. But consequences be damned, we have in our possession what might be the most cutting-edge technology in years, if not decades, and we would be among the first to see it. There is no way I am not going to find out what this is."

"Of course it could just be a bust," I said. "But I have to agree, we can't pass this up. I'm in."

Sylvia was the next to fall in line and declare that she was in. Sylvia probably realized possible risks more than I, and certainly more than Kyle, but part of that mysteriousness about her was that Sylvia had that underlying need to know. There was no way she was going to be left out on something that could be big. Maybe it was just simple curiosity like Kyle and I had or maybe she had some ulterior motive thinking that whatever this was could advance her in some way. But either way, she was in.

This left Larry. When things in life are ones that Larry fully understands and comprehends he can be surprisingly outgoing, but this was not one of those cases.

"Could we get in trouble? Could we get hurt? Could we get kicked out of school?"

None of us answered immediately, as none of us wanted to admit to either Larry or ourselves out loud that any of those was a possibility. Eventually Kyle started to speak, but I stopped him. I knew he would be far less tactful than I, so I took up the mantle.

"Look, Larry. None of us know what is going to happen here. I doubt we can get in real trouble or get kicked out just by turning this on. And it's only a computer and a projector, how could it be dangerous?"

Larry eventually came around and said he was in for at least trying it.

I would be proven very wrong about my last statement.

Chapter 3

Kyle and I agreed that if we were going to go all the way, we would just plug in the projector, turn on the Wi-Fi and start the actual *Oz* program. That seemed to be the main program, and we had no idea how long we might have to run this program before we might be blocked or otherwise shut down. That's assuming it did anything at all in the first place.

We set the projector near the edge of the kitchen table, turning it so it faced a blank white wall about eighteen feet away. We figured that it needed to be that far away to give us a good 'screen'. The power cord was only about six feet long and this setup allowed us to just reach the extra dryer plug on the opposite wall. We turned on the projector first, without it connected to my laptop. It came to life with the hum of cooling fans. No beam projected, but that was to be expected. We figured it probably did not project unless it had a signal. I put my computer on the table, plugged the USB cord from the projector into it, turned on the Wi-Fi, took a deep breath and clicked on the *Oz* icon.

Synching…

That was all the screen said for several moments. We were running the network monitoring tool in the background, and plenty of traffic was flying back and forth.

Local database not found
Updating database…

This went on for a while. We looked into the folder structure and could see that the *Oz Data* directory was filling up with all sorts of files, so we knew something was being sent. All of this was taking place on a stark black and white command line interface. No fancy graphics, splashy logo screens or GUI interfaces. Just a simple blinking cursor.

Finally after what seemed like forever, but was probably about five minutes we got something.

> *Database updated*
> *1) Start Oz*
> *2) Sync Data Files*

"Hmm," I murmured, "I think we just got the latest data files. Should we try sync first anyway?"

Kyle nodded in agreement. At this point he and I were making the decisions as Larry and Sylvia deferred to our geek expertise. Spyrius is known for its fancy interfaces, and for most of their advanced programs I could just say, 'Start Oz' or flick my hand at that option to select it, or at the very least use my mouse. But this was very much old school. It took me a moment before I realized I actually had to use the keyboard.

"I think you actually have to press the number."

"Yes Kyle, I know…" and I pressed '2'.

> *Database current*
> *1) Start Oz*
> *2) Sync Data Files*

"Okay, here we go," I said as I pressed '1'.

> *Welcome to Oz*
> *Select Entry Point*
> *01) Town Square*
> *02) Yorke House*
> *03) Westminster*
> *04) Whitehall*
> *05) Smithfield*
> *06) Highgate*
> *07) Hampton Court*

08) Royal Mews
09) Greenwich
10) Hyde Park
11) Wembley
12) Stratford
13) Kelvedon Hatch Nuclear Bunker

"Kelvedon Hatch Nuclear Bunker?"

I think we all said that at the same time. It didn't take a genius to figure out the running theme, but Sylvia was the first to point it out.

"Everything I recognize on here is in London, I have been there several times."

"Well thank you captain obvious," noted Kyle in a bit of a condescending manner. Sylvia and I gave him a bit of a dirty look. One of the good things about Kyle is that he tries not to be condescending to those not as smart as him, which is just about everyone. In fact he often apologizes for being so smart and tries to come off as being as normal as he can, part of his low self-esteem, even though it rarely works.

"What? It's an expression."

When none of us responded, he elected a humble, "Sorry…"

Larry looked up from his laptop. "Yep, Kelvedon Hatch Nuclear Bunker is right outside London, and everything else is in London. Except 'Town Square'. That seems a bit generic."

"Okay, well which should we try first," I said querying the room, "And no, we should probably not start with Kelvedon Hatch Nuclear Bunker." I said that to Kyle, who I knew would want to go with the oddest first.

Of course we had no idea what *Oz* exactly was. Was it a game, some guide to London, or something we couldn't even conceive?

"Try Wembley, that's where the stadium is," Larry suggested, referring to the iconic football stadium. Seemed like as good a start as any so I pressed '11'. After a few seconds:

> *Wembley currently in use and locked. Try another area.*
> *Select Entry Point*
> *01) Town Square*
> *02) Yorke House*
> *03) Westminster*
> *04) Whitehall*
> *05) Smithfield*
> *06) Highgate*
> *07) Hampton Court*
> *08) Royal Mews*
> *09) Greenwich*
> *10) Hyde Park*
> *11) Wembley*
> *12) Stratford*
> *13) Kelvedon Hatch Nuclear Bunker*

"Well if we can't do the Nuclear Bunker, let's try Greenwich." This time it was Kyle suggesting. "That's a suitably geeky place as it's where all time zones are based off of."

Seemed good to me, so I pressed '09'. Then things got weird.

> *Greenwich available*

The projector hummed as it came to life and the fan speeded up. But instead of projecting an image from the lamp a tiny laser beam shot out. The beam was hidden right under the main lens; none of us actually noticed it before. The beam fanned out, sweeping back and forth across the floor about six feet in front of the projector.

> *Confirming area for door*

The laser stopped.

Area suitable

The projector bulb switched on with an almost blinding light that filled the room. But instead of an image projecting on the far wall, something far more unusual happened leaving all four of us speechless. This machine projected, in the middle of the room about six feet from the projector, a purple three dimensional rectangular object. It was about six feet high by two and a half feet wide by six inches deep. It seemed to shimmer with an almost translucent light and looked in a way like a hologram, but yet at the same time nothing like one.

Door ready

The four of us moved back from the table slowing walking around this object, but not getting too close. We had to squint at first, but slowly our eyes got used to the brightness of the light. We all looked at each other, none of us wanting to be the first to suggest anything, but all of us aware of the last thing we saw on the computer screen.

"A door?"

"Yes Kyle, it said door," I answered.

"What kind of door?" asked Sylvia. "This is no door I have ever seen."

Kyle grabbed a broom that was lying against the wall and slowly reached out to touch the purple door, monolith or whatever it was with the butt end of the broom. He slowly lowered the handle until it just rested on it, where it stayed balanced against the shimmering thing. Then he applied a little pressure, and to our combined amazement the broom handle went right through, surprising Kyle so that he dropped the broom and it fell into the object. This thing was only about six inches thick, yet about two feet of the broom handle went in.

I quickly looked behind, but there was no sign of the broom handle, it had vanished within this thing, whatever it was. Kyle quickly reached down, grabbed the broom and pulled it back. It came back in one piece, not smoking, not scarred, no worse for wear. Kyle tentatively touched the butt end that went into the monolith, and he declared that it felt totally normal.

"I think we know why it's called a door," said Larry stating the obvious.

Kyle put the broom handle in a few more times, now firmly holding on. He waved it around and pulled it in and out. Nothing changed, the broom handle was just fine. So being the impulsive Kyle he volunteered, "Should I put my hand through it and see what happens?"

"No," Larry yelled immediately. "I mean we don't know a thing about this, just because the broom is fine we have no idea what would happen to you. It could be electrified."

"Hold on," I mused. "Let's try a few other things first and see what happens, maybe something metal, something organic…"

We put a hot dog on the end of a stick and put it through, tried a piece of steel to see if there would be any sparks (wrapped in a jacket just in case it was electrified) and even filled a balloon we had, for some reason, with water and tied it to a stick to see if it would get crushed or pop. Everything we put in came back out just fine.

"Shame we don't have a gerbil or rat or something to send through," I said.

"My camera!" exclaimed Sylvia. And that was an excellent idea. Sylvia had one of those sports video cameras that you can clamp on a helmet or a bike handle. She clamped it on to the end of the broom handle, started it recording and put it through the shimmering door waving it around at all angles to get a good view. After about a minute of recording she took it out. Sylvia popped the memory card out and put it into Larry's computer to get a better view. We all gathered around as Larry opened the file.

We all watched as the camera came closer to the purple mass. When it entered the picture became fuzzy, as if it was in a cloud and was accompanied by a slight cracking sound. And then it broke through. On the computer screen was a perfectly clear image of a room, well, more like a storefront actually. It was a medium sized room with picture windows and a door about 20 feet in front of where the camera broke through just like the front of a store. Beyond the windows was a street, just like one would expect outside of a store of any town in the US, or in England as the case may be. As the camera moved left and right there were a couple of free standing wooden counters and a couple of chairs, but that was about it. There was a ceiling about eight feet up and a wooden floor. We obviously could not see what was behind what we assumed was a similar type of 'door' in this other place. What was obvious to all of us was how empty the area was. There were no items in the place, nothing outside the windows, no sounds and no people. It was very surreal.

We wondered if what we were seeing was even real, as none of us could figure out a logical explanation for this.

"Look, I'm just going to rest my finger on that purple thing, that's all, nothing more," Kyle hesitantly said as he slowly moved toward the thing waiting to see if anyone would object. But no one did. In a way I think we were all in a subtle form of shock and no one could think of a reason not to try. So Kyle put his finger against the object, and held it there for a moment.

"Well…?" the three of us asked.

"I feel a slight vibration, very slight, but it is there."

Kyle slowly moved his finger up to the knuckle into the object and then pulled it out. It seemed to be no worse for wear. He then tried a couple more times, each time going in a little farther, each time pulling back out and each time with no ill effects.

"I have to push a little to actually break the plane so to speak, but once in it's easy to go through. The thing is denser than air, but not as dense as, say, water. I can feel a slight buzz like there is a mild current going through, but very slight."

The last time Kyle put his whole arm in, all the way to his biceps. "I've broken through; I don't feel the slight buzzing on my hand any more, it's only about a six inch slice where I can feel anything."

By now Kyle had his arm back out and was looking at it as if he was trying to find anything wrong or unusual. But he could not. After a few minutes of us all staring at Kyle's totally normally looking arm he put his arm to his side and took a deep breath.

"One of us has to go through."

Kyle is normally the impulsive one, but there was just something about this that made me believe it was safe and more importantly that I wanted to be the first one of us to actually go through. It's one of those moments where you just know that whatever happens this is a life changing moment, one of those crossroads, grab the bull by the horns and don't look back kind of moments…

"I'm going through," I announced.

Kyle gave me a hurt look that asked why I was trying to deny him the chance when he was the logical choice to go through first.

"You're too impetuous Kyle," I firmly stated. "You may be the smartest of us, but we need someone a little more careful, who can logically analyze the situation and factor in the risk to reward ratio. And while yes, Larry is the most analytic of us in first analyzing the situation, he is a little too risk adverse. We need a good balance, and I am it."

I think Kyle was a little taken aback by the firmness of my stance. Personally I was too, it was like I needed to sway the constituents to vote for my position.

"And where do I fit in?" asked Sylvia, perhaps feeling a little left out.

"You would be a good fit too, but I am still more the techie geek, and this thing, whatever it might be, is very techie geek."

Larry and Sylvia nodded as if they were fine with me being the first through. Kyle was not happy and looked like he considered for a moment just making a run for the purple mass. In the end he decided that there were too many risks even for him. With a hurt look on his face he retreated to the couch to sulk.

"I think we need to take a few precautions first," Larry said. "If you're going through that thing we need to at least tie a rope around your waist so we can pull you back if anything happens. And I want you to wear Sylvia's camera, plugged into my laptop on this side at least at first. I have a ten foot USB cable we can use, and you should not go any farther the first time."

"Does anyone actually have some rope?" I asked.

We all looked at each other, except for Kyle, who was just sulking, and came to the conclusion that none of us had rope.

"Give me a second," Sylvia said. "I think the building super might have some." And with that she headed out.

Meanwhile Larry and I fastened Sylvia's camera to a headband and put it on my head with a cable running to Larry's laptop. While waiting for Sylvia I basically repeated what Kyle did, putting first my finger and then my whole arm through the shimmering door. It was just like Kyle said, a very slight buzzing feel, like a small electrical current while actually going through the door itself, but other than that, nothing.

Kyle was still sulking, having not said a word. I was pretty used to this slight manic-depressive behavior and I knew as soon as something started to happen Kyle would be right back into things. Larry noticed too.

"Kyle, I'm going to need you to monitor the laptop and watch and listen to what's happening with Josh. I'm going to be anchoring the rope, ready to pull him back if necessary."

"Whatever."

"Come on Kyle, you're going to have to monitor me and give the word if Larry needs to pull me back. I'm putting my life in your hands," I said with slight exaggeration for effect.

"Yeah, good enough to monitor your life, but not good enough to share a place with."

I just sighed.

For as much as Kyle and I get along, we get on each other's nerves… a lot. We always have. Usually we can get away from each other for a bit and by the next day we are fine. One of my dad's pieces of advice when Kyle and I were first getting ready for college was that we should not share a dorm room together as we would end up killing each other and it would be the end of our friendship. My dad actually likes Kyle but he realized that we wouldn't have the space from each other we needed if we were sharing a room. Kyle bought the reasoning and I am convinced that if we had shared a room together last year one of us would have been killed by the other by now, or at least it would have done real damage to our friendship. Kyle wanted us to get a place together this year, but I didn't want to fix what was not broken. Not wanting to get into an argument I sneakily got the place with Larry and Sylvia all set before breaking the news to Kyle. He was furious and hurt beyond anything I had ever seen before. His point was that if we could not manage to share an apartment with separate bedrooms then we weren't really good friends, pointing out that I basically wanted to have my cake and to eat it too. Ultimately I had to admit this was true, and I had to promise him that after this year, for our junior and senior years we would get a place together. This smoothed things over for the rest of summer, but I think actually coming down to school where Larry, Sylvia and I were in our own place, while he was still stuck back in the dorms, brought all the bad feelings back.

"Look I said I was sorry, can't we just put that to rest? You are right, I was wrong, and I will make it up to you. But right now we have the coolest thing that will probably never happen to either of us in our lives right in front of us. Come on!"

Just then Sylvia came back with package of rope, actually a package labeled clothesline.

"Nobody hangs clothes on a clothesline anymore," she observed.

"All right, let's do this." That came from Kyle who, after a bit of processing, decided he was back into this adventure.

The clothesline worked just fine. Kyle and Larry wrapped it around my waist and through both legs like a climber's harness, leaving about 10 feet, double-wrapped for strength, behind me for Larry to hold on to.

We were all set. Larry was behind me holding on to the rope. The camera was attached to my head with a cable running from it to the laptop in Kyle's lap as he sat on a chair right next to me a few inches from the door. Sylvia was standing off to the side with her cell phone acting as a video camera recording the whole proceeding for posterity, or for the police investigation if I ended up dead.

"Alright, I'm going to stick my head through, just enough to get to the other side. I'm going to keep my left hand out here with my thumb up. If it falls for any reason you pull me back."

"Got it," said Larry as it pulled up the flack on the rope so it was taut.

I put my left arm to the side with my thumb up and stared at the purple thing only an inch or so in front of me and then realized I was terrified. A hand and arm was one thing, but my head, my mind? We still had no idea what this thing even was or what might happen. I thought this was probably like what Neil Armstrong felt when he was ready to open the Eagle lunar module to set foot on the Moon for the first time. No one really knew what would be there or what would happen, it was a leap of faith for the sake of exploration. I tried to think logically that this was a Spyrius device that obviously was meant for this. Or at least I hoped so. Either way I wasn't going to chicken out now. If nothing else Kyle would never let me live it down after I insisted that I go first over him. I gave a quick look over to him and I think even he realized there was a certain real risk in what I was doing. He smiled, reached out and gave my right hand a quick squeeze. I closed my eyes, took a deep breath, held it and pushed my head in.

I felt the slight buzzing, no different than when I put my arm through. After a moment I felt the buzzing only on my neck and top of my shoulders and I knew my head was through. I could still feel the muscles in my left hand holding up my arm and I gave a little shake so they would know I was okay. I opened my eyes. What I saw was exactly what we saw when we sent the video camera through. It looked like a storefront, and it looked as real as anything else I've ever seen. The air was still and the temperature seemed normal room temperature. What didn't seem real was the lack of any life. There was no movement, and more strikingly, no sound. And I mean none. Almost anywhere in today's society there is some background noise somewhere, something I don't think I ever realized until that moment, where the lack of sound was almost deafening. Certainly something noticeable.

Up to this point I had been holding my breath, not sure if there would be breathable air. Before I could analyze anything else I had to take into account that my brain was sending signals telling me that I better breathe soon or it was going to do it for me. So I took just a quick little breath through my nose. Everything seemed okay. So I took a bigger breath. The air seemed very clean. I took a few more controlled breaths and everything seemed okay.

Though I could not hear my friends outside, the camera on my head had microphones, so I figured that they should be able to hear me. I spoke out "hello?" in a normal speaking volume. There was no reply.

"If you can hear me, Kyle, I am going to put my right foot through and test the floor."

While the storefront looked solid enough I had not actually touched any objects yet. The position I was in, hunched over with my legs behind me, holding my left hand out was starting to get a bit uncomfortable. I wanted to at least test the floor before I left so I swung my right leg through and firmly placed it on the floor. Larry had a solid grip on the rope which I could feel pulling back on me, so even if my foot when through the floor I would not lose my balance. But it didn't. It stopped on the wooden floor just like I hoped, making the sound of a foot being placed on a wooden floor just like one would expect. I gave a few quick stomps and everything seemed normal, or at least the floor seemed solid.

With my right foot solidly on the ground inside the door I was able to turn around and look behind me. As I expected I looked right at a big purple shimmering monolith just like the one in our room. I couldn't look far enough around to see if there was a similar projector but figured I could leave that for another time. It was time to come back out, and so I did.

Chapter 4

Fully back in the dorm room, I instinctively put my hands to my face just to make sure nothing changed.

"You look just as ugly as you always have," Larry said.

I took my hands away, not even sure why I did that.

"Well?" asked Kyle.

"It seemed fine," I said. "Did you see and hear everything in the video?"

Kyle nodded in the affirmative. Sylvia was still filming the whole thing on her cell phone.

"Okay then, let me walk fully into that room still hooked up with the rope and camera," and then, before Kyle could get out what I knew was coming, "and then we'll hook you up and you can go through."

"Sounds good," he said with a smile.

On my second venture I just walked straight through the door and into the other side. I was limited by how far I could go, not just by the rope but by the USB cable snaking back to the laptop. I was able to go far enough to reach out and touch a counter, which felt solid and normal, as did the floor itself when I squatted down and touched it. The purple door behind me had the same dimensions as the one in our apartment, and I could walk just far enough to look around. Here's where I got my first surprise: behind the door was more counter space and the back wall, but there was no projector creating the door. It was just freestanding. I thought perhaps there was a power source under the floor that it was resting on so I got on my knees and ran my hand along the bottom of the door. It felt solid all the way through, no obvious power source. That quandary would have to wait for later. I went back through the door and came out in our apartment figuring I had done all I could for this excursion.

Kyle was itching to go through at this point. I think part of me wanted to protect him like a big brother but I could see no real reason to put it off any longer. I did insist on him being hooked up the same way I was with the rope and the video camera hooked to the laptop. He agreed and went through, doing basically the same things I did, as there wasn't much else to do with the limited reach of the USB cable and rope.

When Kyle came back we knew we needed to analyze what we had discovered and figure out what to do next. It was Sylvia that came up with one of the more interesting insights.

"So, Josh and Kyle, correct me if I am wrong but the laptop powering this projector and door, or whatever it is, is connected to the Internet, right?"

"Yes," we both answered.

"And it's connected back to Spyrius, correct?"

"Yes," I answered, and both Kyle and I were coming around to what Sylvia was getting at. Kyle went to my laptop to check the traffic.

"So what's to stop them from knowing what we are doing?"

"There is traffic going to and from Spyrius," Kyle stated from behind my laptop. "It's being sent encrypted over SSL but we can see the unencrypted data from our side. Hold on. Yeah, it's just gibberish, or more precisely it's data in some format that we have no knowledge of, but there is definitely data going back from here to them. Not a huge amount, but something is going back to them."

I continued the thread, "So we can assume there is at least a strong possibility that they know that we have this thing on."

"Considering how eager they were to get this room back, offering us ten thousand dollars cash, and considering this is some sort of portal to another place, I would think that they would care a lot," Larry added.

"Yep, they could be coming up the stairs right now," I said.

"I'm an idiot!" exclaimed Kyle

"Annoying yes, but idiot, no," Sylvia interjected. "I'll bite though, why are you an idiot?"

"I should have sent the traffic through an anonymous proxy."

"I don't think that would have mattered much, Kyle," I mused. "There are probably very few of these projector things and they already know we are in their room. I would think they could put two and two together pretty fast."

"What is an anonymous proxy?" Larry asked.

"It's a way to send Internet traffic through a third party that keeps the true origin, in this case us, anonymous," I answered. "Though in reality there is no such thing as anonymous Internet usage at all, but done properly it can really slow down someone trying to find you."

"We barely scratched the surface of this thing. This is the most amazing thing I have ever seen or experienced. We have to go in and explore this world!" Kyle said with the excitement of a kid in a candy factory. "I am not about to give this thing up!"

"Hold your horses there, manic one," Larry said to Kyle. "We have no idea what that place through that weird door even is, or what would happen if someone turned off the projector while you were in there. There is way too much risk here. Maybe we should call Spyrius and tell them what we found."

"Kyle's right for once. We need to explore, and we need to do it somewhere else."

"Sylvia?" questioned Larry.

"Sorry Larry, but this is just too cool. And stop looking at me that way. What, only the two geeks can have fun? I want to go in there too."

"Over my dead body!"

"Thank you for your genuine concern about my health, Laurence." (You can tell Sylvia is being sarcastic when she calls Larry Laurence) "But I fully intend to explore in this thing."

"But where else could we go with this?" I asked.

"My house," said Sylvia. "I only live an hour away and my parents left this morning for their European vacation."

"Are you insane?" Larry was raising his voice at this time. "Ignoring how much legal trouble we might get into, we have no idea if this thing is the least bit safe. What, do you expect the four of us to just go strolling in there like are taking a Sunday afternoon walk on campus?"

The three of us looked at each other for a moment before we looked back at Larry and answered, almost in unison, "Yes."

We couldn't get Larry to change his mind on the danger and stupidity of the whole thing, but we did come to an agreement that if we were to continue further we should move to Sylvia's house before doing anything else.

First we needed to shut down the system. The screen on the computer still showed:

Door Ready

"Try Control-C," said Kyle referencing a common command to break out of a command line program.

That didn't work.

"Maybe it really is obvious," I said as I hit 'Q' for Quit.

Are you sure you want to quit (Y/N)?

I pressed 'Y'.

Checking Door
Oz Clear
Closing Door

And with that the projector shut off and the purple door disappeared.

"*Oz Clear*. I wonder what that means," pondered Kyle to himself.

The hour-long drive to Sylvia's parents' house was pretty uneventful. We stopped for food at a fast food place off of I-81 for dinner, but mostly it was just a quiet drive as we all were into our own thoughts, trying to make sense of what just happened and what we were going to do. Larry, who was driving Sylvia's car, kept muttering under his breath how stupid this all was. The rest of us ignored him. In fact the only memorable part was carrying the projector from our room to the car, as it took both Larry and I to carry it, and we almost dropped it at one point.

It was getting dark when we arrived at the nondescript colonial in the nondescript typical American post-war suburb outside of Roanoke, Virginia, where Sylvia and her family lived. The house was built in the late Sixties, though it had gone through a few upgrades over the decades to make it a little more modern. One upgrade was to move the washer/dryer, originally in the basement, up to a small room on an expanded second floor, which we would need for its 240 volt outlet.

Sylvia has an older sister who just went off to her senior year at University of Virginia, who I have never met, and with whom Sylvia does not have the greatest relationship. "She's a stuck up arrogant jerk," would be typical of Sylvia's opinion of her sister. Last year her parents took advantage of having both daughters out of the house for the first time to take a month-long trip to Europe. They did the same thing this year, which left the house empty.

I have a sister too, but she is younger by two years. Her name is Sydney and we get along good enough, though we really don't have anything in common. Larry has a couple of older brothers and a sister, I think. Not really sure, but they are all way older than he is. Larry was one of those happy accidents. Kyle, as mentioned before, is an only child, though my parents have grudgingly accepted him into our family so he can experience all those mundane things like family dinners at a casual dining restaurant or a summer evening at a baseball game. Things that Kyle's parents would never do.

Larry and I set the projector up on the dryer itself, which we surmised would give just enough room for the door to be projected while still allowing us to walk around it. Kyle was in charge of setting up my computer, on the washer, so that all the traffic ran through an anonymous proxy. Since the *Oz* application didn't have an obvious setting to use a proxy he just set it up so all traffic would go through the anonymous proxy. This was a little beyond my knowledge, I would have had to figure it out, but to Kyle it was a piece of cake. Meanwhile Sylvia put a nice dark blanket over the window that looked out to the front of the house so all the neighbors wouldn't see a blinding light coming from the laundry room.

"We haven't really given much thought to what we are going to actually do," I said.

"Larry," Sylvia said turning to her boyfriend. "You don't want to go in, right?" Larry nodded in the affirmative. "So why don't you stay here and make sure everything goes okay on this end?"

"And pray tell what am I going to do if you don't come back out?"

"Then you have my permission to call Spyrius!" Kyle exclaimed.

Larry did not take that well, and spent the next few minutes trying talk all of us, but mostly Sylvia out of doing this. In the end we decided that we would stay within line of sight of the door at all times in this first real foray. We also decided to try Greenwich again, leaving others for another time.

"You know," Kyle mused, "we also need to figure out what that *Oz Creator* program is. If it's what I am thinking…"

"One thing at a time buddy…" and as I trailed off with my comment, while picking the same choices as last time, the projector came to life and a new purple door, portal, whatever was created in Sylvia's parents laundry room.

"First let's make sure things look and work the same as they did before," I remarked.

"Sure," said Kyle, "but let me do it this time. I'll be methodical, I promise!"

I agreed and Kyle went through a similar routine as before. He first put his hand through, then his head, then his legs, and came back saying everything looked exactly the same as it did last time. The only odd thing he said was that it was a little harder to go through, like the portal was slightly denser. After a few more tries everything seemed to work okay, so we didn't worry about it.

Having somehow taken a leadership role here, I said that Kyle would go through first, then Sylvia, wearing her camera on a headband to record the proceedings, and then I would take up the rear. We would stay within sight of the door and be gone no more than 15 minutes, though we really never came to an agreement of what Larry should do if we didn't come back within that time. So Kyle went through, after I made him promise that he would wait within three feet of the door and not wander. Sylvia then gave Larry a really intimate hug and kiss like I have rarely seen them do before.

"I'll be back," she said to Larry as she walked toward the door. But then she froze.

The doorbell rang.

Chapter 5

"What do we do?" Sylvia whispered.

"Carefully peak out the windows and see what's up," I said, also in a whisper.

"I don't see anything out of the ordinary, but I can't see the front door from here."

"Well then we probably should answer it. Remember, no one is supposed to be here and we don't want a nosy neighbor calling the cops."

"Okay, but tell Kyle to come back."

Sylvia went downstairs and I poked my head through the door. Kyle looked puzzled and a little concerned, but I told him what happened and he came back out for the moment.

"Everything seems exactly the same as last time," he noted.

We could hear Sylvia talking to someone, and it seemed lighthearted so we all breathed a sigh of relief that someone from Spyrius had not followed us here.

"Yep," Sylvia said when she came back. "It was Mrs. Barry who lives next door. My parents asked them to keep an eye on the house. I told them I forgot something important and that we would probably just stay the night here. So we are in the clear for now."

"Good job," I said.

"So are we ready to try this again?" asked Kyle.

I gave him the thumbs up and he went through. Sylvia just smiled at Larry, put her arm through first to test things out and then walked through the door. I told Larry we would see him shortly and then walked on through.

Unfettered by the rope, and with the camera free from the restraints of the USB cable, we could fully explore the 'storefront' that we were in. It was pretty much all made from wood, with wood floors, tables, chairs and wood counters. The walls looked like normal plaster or drywall painted a very bland grey. An open door in the back led to a small storeroom with some generic metal shelving and off to the side of that room was a small bathroom. The feeling was like something out of the American old west, though the bathroom fixtures and metal shelving were more modern. The oddest thing though, was that except for the big purple door in the middle of the main room there was nothing more than the furniture and counters. The place was empty, but not just in the lack of items but empty in its feel. No sound, no bugs, no dust, no air circulation. The fluorescent lighting coming from the ceiling didn't even make the slight buzzing sound one sometimes hears. The whole place seemed brand new and totally lifeless.

Then there was the purple door. There was no projector; it was just there. The back side that was bathed in the projector light in our version had a slightly darker sheen to it, and you could not stick anything through it. We tried with a pen Sylvia had. It was solid on that side.

"There was a roll of toilet paper in the bathroom," Sylvia noted.

"Really," I said having not noticed the first time. I went back and sure enough a full roll was on the holder. Curious, I turned on the sink and water flowed like normal. I even flushed the toilet, and it flushed though, being the only sound, it seemed twice as loud as normal.

Back in the main room Kyle was examining the vents.

"It's perfectly normal room temperature, but there is no air coming from the vents," he noted. "This place just seems so sterile, so dead."

"Don't say that word!" Sylvia tersely said.

"Sorry."

Walking to the front of the store we could get a much better look outside the windows. There was a sidewalk and then an asphalt road, though not very wide, and then a row of identical one-story wooden 'storefronts' that looked just like the one we were in, but without a purple door inside that we could see. Looking up, the sky looked blue. There was light as if it was mid-day, but I could not see any sun or light source from our angle within the store.

Up to that point the three of us were just wandering in a kind of daze, soaking everything in, but I realized we had to take some action.

"Okay, what time is it?" I asked.

We all pulled out our phones which showed 7:04 pm.

"Well it definitely does not look like 7:04 out there," I said pointing out the storefront windows. Either way we need to go back through the portal by 7:15 at the latest."

"Is that what we are going to call it?" Sylvia asked.

"Call what?"

"The purple door thingy we came through, are we calling it a portal?"

"Oh, I guess," I said, not even realizing I said that. "I guess that's a better name than door, and this way we won't confuse it with real doors."

"Spyrius calls it a door in the program," Kyle said looking up from his phone, "but I agree, portal seems much more apropos."

"Shall we try walking out the door of this store?" I asked. "We just need to stay within line of sight of the portal."

"Sure," Sylvia responded.

"Holy…!" exclaimed Kyle still working on his phone.

"What?" both Sylvia and I asked.

"So there is no cell reception from in here, and no GPS reception, but get this, there are two Wi-Fi hotspots, and they are labeled - you're not going to believe this - *Greenwich*, which has a strong signal, and *Hyde Park*, which has a weak signal. Oh wait, *Royal Mews* came in just for a second, real faint, but now it's gone."

"Well the names makes sense," I said, "Those are the place names for portals. But do you see anything in this place that looks like networking equipment? I don't."

"And I'll tell you another thing," Sylvia said, "They may have names from London, but this place looks nothing like London!"

"Can you connect?" I asked.

"No, it requires a WEP key," Kyle responded and then added looking at Sylvia, "That's the networking password."

"I know, I've set up Wi-Fi before," Sylvia said sounding slightly annoyed.

We went out the store's front door, first making sure it didn't lock behind us, and ventured out onto the small sidewalk before the normal looking street. Looking to the left and right there were some cross streets at odd angles. Though everything felt solid and real, the whole place just felt, well, unreal. Every storefront was exactly the same. Colors were a little different and doors might be in different places, but architecturally they were all the same model. The sky was just a monochromatic, muted shade of blue, with no sun or obvious light source. As in the store there was no sign of life, no breeze, no sounds. From a certain point on the street we could see some bigger buildings way in the distance. There were a few brick office buildings that were probably four stories and the tallest building looked like a church, complete with a steeple and church bell.

"This road looks brand new," Sylvia noted. "It doesn't look like a car has ever driven on it."

Kyle was lying flat on the road with a puzzled look on his face. He got up, looked around a bit, and then made an observation that only Kyle would.

"This isn't a real road. There is no drainage."

"Explain yourself please."

"Well, Sylvia, all roads in any city are slightly curved from the center down to the edges so that rain drains to the gutters and down into a sewer. But this road is dead flat, and there are no drains I can see anywhere."

"But the sink and toilet, they worked," I said, "So there has to be some sort of sewer system. I guess?"

I crossed the street and went up to the store that was directly across from the store we came from. Through the windows it looked exactly the same, sans the big purple portal. I told Kyle to hold the door open while I looked around quickly. It was exactly the same as our original store. The wall colors were slightly different and the wood a different shade, but essentially it was a duplicate.

We are all standing in the road when I looked at my phone and realized that it was 7:13.

"We need to get back," I said. "We can try to make sense of this back at Sylvia's and figure out what to do next."

"Sound good," Kyle responded. "I think going to the church would be the next logical move. That seems like a city center, or something like that."

"I'll bet you that's Town Square," Sylvia remarked.

We went back to the shop we came from and all three of us went back through the portal. We appeared right back in Sylvia's laundry room, no worse for wear.

"About time. I was starting to get a little worried," Larry said with a slight, but definite note of anger in his voice.

"Okay, Kyle," said Sylvia after we all sat down at the kitchen table. "You are the genius, and I'm not being sarcastic time. What is your analysis of what is going on here?"

You could see the synapses firing about in Kyle's brain as he considered everything that we had experienced so far.

"Let's analyze what we have here. First we have to assume that this is not some mass hypnosis, and we have to suspend belief in everything we thought we knew about how things work and make the assumption that this does exist. This is some sort of portal that physically transfers you to another world of some sort, but I am pretty sure that this world is not fully real."

"Felt real to me," I said.

"Quiet. I am on a roll here," Kyle chided. "It's real in the fact that we can touch things and breathe, but it don't think it's real as in organically created like the Earth. I think 'Oz,' which we might as well call it, is a technological creation from Spyrius."

"How?" Sylvia asked, obviously quite interested in what Kyle said.

"That I don't know. Think about it this way: when the Wright Brothers and the other pioneer aviators first took to the sky and flew over a farm in Nebraska or somewhere, that farmer probably thought it was the work of the devil or something. In other words only the very few people who were actually working on creating an airplane could even conceive of a mechanical flying machine as a real possibility. To the vast majority of people it wasn't even conceivable. I mean, if you asked an average person in 1949 if they thought humans would walk on the Moon in 20 years you know what kind of an answer you would get."

"Wasn't Galileo thrown in jail for saying the Earth revolved around the Sun?" I added.

"Umm, yeah Josh, close enough analogy. The point is that obviously Spyrius has been working on a technology that allows a person to be transported, for lack of a better word, through this portal thingy into some sort of, what I believe to be, artificial world."

"So what do we do next?" asked Sylvia.

"Explore it, of course!" Kyle answered.

"No!" Larry said with a bang of his fist on the table.

Up to that point Larry had been sitting there very quietly with only a scowl on his face. But now he got up and faced Kyle with a hint of menace in his voice, surprising for the normally laid back Larry.

"I've put up with your impulsive antics enough, Kyle. Fine, I will use your own analogy. An early Sopwith Camel lands in a farmer's field. Let's say the pilot died of a heart attack in-flight so he couldn't tell the farmer anything about what the machine is. So the farmer climbs into the plane, turns it on, pulls back on the stick and gets it in the air. What do you think would happen?"

He did not wait for any of us to answer.

"I'll tell you. He will crash and die because he has no training on how to fly a plane, no conception of how pitch and yaw work, and no inkling of what to do. Instead the farmer should have tried to call the plane's owner and have them come and retrieve the plane. Heck maybe the poor farmer might even get a reward from the plane's owner. Oh wait, that's right, we could have gotten ten grand if we had given Spyrius back what was obviously supposed to be their apartment in the first place."

"You have to manually turn the props to start the planes back, then…"

I cringed as Kyle said that. He really didn't know when not to push people's buttons.

"It's a damn analogy, idiot. I've sat here biting my tongue while you were exploring this, whatever it is, but enough is enough. The point is none of us have any idea what is really going on with this thing, and I am not about to let my girlfriend go back in it."

Oops. I knew that was going to be a problem. Larry and Sylvia truly love each other, but as I stated earlier, while Larry *thinks* he runs the relationship, he most definitely does not. Sylvia is very strong willed, but most of the time she lets Larry think he's the one making the decisions. She will make an excellent psychology student and an excellent lawyer. One thing I know about Sylvia is that she will not stand for Larry, or anyone for that matter, telling her what she can or cannot do. It didn't matter that Larry's statement had its basis in genuine love and concern for her, coupled with his own fear of the unknown, Sylvia was going to do what she damn well pleased.

It was pretty obvious that Larry realized this immediately as he stopped talking and Sylvia stood up.

"Larry, I think you and I need to have a short discussion privately."

With that, Larry and Sylvia headed upstairs, though not until she requested that Kyle not go into the portal until they were back.

"Okay," I said to Kyle. "Just to play devil's advocate here, what do you think of Larry's point? Because it's actually not an unreasonable analogy. I'm sure the Spyrius people have a full understanding of how this all works and what the dos and don'ts are."

"So, your point? Okay, even the impetuous side of me can take a back seat to logic for a moment, but even if he has a point are you willing to give up the chance to experience what might be the greatest technological breakthrough of the century at the ground floor?"

I didn't actually answer him, mostly because I was trying to see if I could figure out a reason not to want to go in. I was terrified for just a moment when I first put my head through the portal, but other than that nothing seemed out of the realm of what we could comfortably control.

"Let me put it this way," Kyle said to me. "If I gave you a chance to go on a rocket into space right now, just for the chance to be in outer space, would you take it?"

"Yeah, no question."

"Yet if you add up all the people who have been in space and divide by all the people killed in space or spaceflight-related incidents there is like a two or three percent chance you will die. Yet many people would gladly take that risk without thought to experience something so phenomenal. And so far we have seen nothing to give us any indication that our lives are in danger in there. In fact I am making the assumption that Spyrius built this to be as safe as possible."

And with that I think Kyle actually swayed me with a logical reason as to why the reward of continuing our exploration of Oz was greater than any possible unknown risk. It would be later when I would find out that this line of thinking was very naïve.

"While we are waiting for Sylvia to calm down Larry, let's go take a look at that *Oz Creator* program. I have a feeling that may give us a lot of insights as to what this all is."

I agreed and we went back up to the laundry room, yelling out to Sylvia that we were just going to poke around on the computer so she didn't think we were going back into Oz.

We disconnected my laptop from the projector and brought it into the guest bedroom next to the laundry room, as it had a desk we could put the laptop on. We started the since-neglected *Oz Creator* program.

> *Synching…*
> *Updating database…*
> *Database current*
> *Select a Section to Edit*
> *01) Town Square*
> *02) Yorke House*
> *03) Westminster*
> *04) Whitehall*
> *05) Smithfield*
> *06) Highgate*
> *07) Hampton Court*
> *08) Royal Mews*
> *09) Greenwich*
> *10) Hyde Park*
> *11) Wembley*
> *12) Stratford*
> *13) Kelvedon Hatch Nuclear Bunker*

"Whoa," I said. "I think you are onto something here, Kyle. This looks like some way of actually editing this world."

"Told you so. We might as well start by picking what we know."

"*Greenwich* it is."

So I selected '09'.

> *Locking Section 'Greenwich'*
> *Checking PC requirements*
> *CPU - Sufficient*
> *Memory - Insufficient*
> *Graphics Card - Insufficient*
> *Monitor Size - Insufficient*
> *Requirements not met*
> *Unlocking Section 'Greenwich'*

And the program exited.

"But my laptop is brand new!" I cried out.

"Why would you program the requirements check after you select the section to edit? You would think they would program it to perform the check first."

"What? Kyle, you think of the oddest things sometimes."

"Well sorry, but that just seems like backward programming. Anyway, yeah, but I bet working on something like this requires the likes of top-of-the-line CAD/CAM workstation. Not a laptop. Damn, I think we could have learned a lot from that program. Now where can we get our hands on a top-of-the-line Spyrius workstation?"

"Nowhere that I know of. Our computer labs don't even have Spyrius machines and I don't have ten grand in my pocket to go buy one."

"Well we could have!" Kyle said jokingly referring to the ten thousand dollars initially offered us by the Spyrius employee. "Of course then we wouldn't need to buy one! Nice Catch-22 there."

At that point Larry and Sylvia came out of Sylvia's room.

"Larry's going to join us for a small excursion to the Town Square area."

Chapter 6

Larry did not look very happy and there was some obvious tension in the air. I have no idea what Sylvia did, but obviously she worked her magic on him. Kyle looked like he was going to say something but I muttered a quick, "don't" to him under my breath and he got the hint. I was not too sure if it was a good idea to have someone who obviously did not really want to go into Oz going in there. It was one thing to convince Larry that it was okay for Sylvia to go in with Kyle and me, he could do a good job monitoring everything outside, but another to make him go in against his will. I was not sure if Sylvia was forcing Larry to go in or if she somehow bullied Larry into it by picking on his manhood. After all Larry was bigger and stronger than either Kyle or me, and if Kyle and I were man enough to go in… Either way I was not about to ask.

"First Larry and I are going to quickly go through the portal into the storefront so Larry can feel comfortable with the whole thing. Fire it up and you two wait here," Sylvia said to me.

I started the *Oz* program, selecting Greenwich as usual. I told Sylvia to hold on a second, the only words spoken by anyone while the program started, and then quickly stuck my head through the portal to make sure everything looked the same. It did, and so Sylvia took Larry's hand and stepped through. With Sylvia through and Larry still on our side, he looked at me and gave me the dirtiest look I think he has ever given me. He was not happy, and with that he went through.

"Wow, what do you think happened there?" Kyle asked me. "You're the psychology expert."

"I took Psychology 101; hardly makes me an expert. I don't know… I have no idea. I do know that I'm not too sure I like Larry being coerced into this."

"Oh, come on. He'll be fine once he realizes that there is no danger and everything is copasetic."

"Maybe, but I'm not too sure. Let's see what happens when they come back out."

After waiting for a few minutes we were starting to wonder what was going on. I was about to stick my head through to check the status of things when Larry came back through with Sylvia right behind him.

Larry still didn't look happy and he was not saying anything, but his body language did not seem as bad as before.

"So," Sylvia said, "if we are going down to the big church, what should we take with us? Besides my camera I was thinking we should have some way of marking where we go so we don't get lost, and I have the perfect solution. I have some of that sidewalk chalk from last year and we can use that to make marks in the road."

"Great idea," I said. Sylvia had some volunteer work with kids as part of her child psychology class last semester so that explained why she had the chalk. "I think we should take a little water and some snacks just in case we get hungry. What else?"

"A flashlight or two," Kyle added. "And that rope we bought, bring that, and the lock pick set, which I still have in my pocket."

"Agreed on the first two, and a writing pad and pens if we have them," I said. "I doubt we will be picking locks though."

"You never know."

"I have a couple of small backpacks," Sylvia stated. "Let me get them and fill them up with some food, chalk, a flashlight each, paper, pens and the rope. I think I still have my Swiss Army Knife. We'll take that along."

I told Kyle to go help Sylvia and they went off to gather the supplies, leaving Larry and me in the room.

"Are you okay, buddy?" I said in as nice, calm and caring a voice as I could without sounding condescending.

"Don't worry about it," he said in an almost defeatist voice.

I didn't want to push things, but I wanted to make sure Larry was at least not going in against his will. Although the two of us got along fine last year and were around each other all the time we never talked about our feelings or anything touchy-feely in nature. There was one night when he was really sick, sweating and throwing up, when I had to mother him a bit. That was the only time he ever told me he that he appreciated me. He never even talked about his and Sylvia's relationship to me; that all came from Sylvia.

"You know you don't have to join us if you don't want to. It's okay."

He looked at me and sighed. "Just don't worry. I'll be fine."

"It will be okay," I said as I smiled and gave him a little playful punch in the arm. It was the best I could think of doing under the circumstances.

He half smiled back. At least enough to alleviate my concern a little. I was relieved that he wasn't scowling at me anymore. To be honest I think he was scared, but I couldn't tell if he was being too concerned or if the rest of us were not concerned enough.

"The thing I don't understand is, why are we doing this in the first place?"

"Well I can't speak for the others, but for me it's simply the sense of adventure. For me, with something like this place in front of me, I can't not go. Kind of like why a spelunker explores a cave or a diver explores a shipwreck."

"Maybe I just don't have that adventure gene that you, Kyle and, I guess it turns out, Sylvia have."

"Maybe. That's why I am saying don't go if you don't really want to. I don't want you hating this and then being mad at me for the rest of the year. You're too good of a roommate."

"Josh, you are nowhere near as naïve as Kyle, but on some things you are. I'm coming, and don't worry I am not mad at you."

With that he walked out of the room to use the bathroom, signaling that was the end of the discussion.

Sylvia and Kyle came back with two backpacks. Each had some water, snacks, chalk, a flashlight, pad of paper and pens. Sylvia had the idea of the buddy system. No matter what, Kyle and I would always stay together and Larry and she would do the same. Each pair had one of the backpacks. Sylvia had her pocketknife and the camera on her head like before. Kyle and I had the rope and, of course, my lock pick set that Kyle was now carrying. If we ever got truly separated, everyone would immediately go back to the Greenwich portal and back to Sylvia's laundry room.

"Do we have everything we need?" Larry asked, trying his best to be part of the team.

"Probably not. I'm sure we will realize we forgot something!" Kyle blurted out and both Sylvia and I just shook our heads.

"I mean, I'm sure we're fine, Larry," Kyle said correcting himself.

"We are not going far," I said. "There has been no indication of anything that would be a problem, and if anything sketchy happens we just immediately trace our steps back and come back here. Sound good?"

With everyone nodding in the affirmative, one backpack on my back, one on Larry's we set off into this place called Oz.

We all went through the portal with no issues and found ourselves in the usual storefront. We went outside to the street and made a right toward the big buildings and the church. Before we went any farther Sylvia took out the chalk and drew a big arrow in the middle of the street turning and pointing to the storefront that the portal was in.

"The purple thing may look obvious, but all these buildings look the same. Better to draw too much…" Sylvia noted.

We all agreed and we walked down to the first intersection. The main intersections that we could see from our vantage point were at odd angles. Instead of nice 90 degree crosses, these streets crossed at 30 or 120 degree angles. It looked more like the random streets of Boston or most European cities rather than the nice crosshatch pattern of Manhattan or Washington D.C. The 'storefronts' at the corners were the same general layout but the corners came to either sharp points or wide obtuse angles. About halfway down the street we were on was a street at a 90 degree angle that looked more like an alley.

"You would think if you were creating an artificial city you would make the streets parallel and perpendicular." Kyle mused.

"Certainly makes it more confusing to get around," Sylvia added.

"Maybe that was the point," Larry observed.

It was nice to see Larry at least adding something to the conversation. While not looking excited about being there, he at least seemed to mellow back into his old self for the moment. Meanwhile Kyle had his hand on his chin and was staring toward the alley at something. When I saw what he was looking at I proceeded to steal his idea.

"That street faces the back of buildings, and there are ladders that lead up to the roof. I say we go up and take a look."

Kyle looked at me with the most incredulous look on his face.

"Just for the record, it was Kyle's idea. I just stole it before he could say anything," I said so not to annoy my friend.

Indeed, catty-corner to where we were was a smaller alleyway that faced the backs of the buildings. As we walked toward the alley, Sylvia drawing her chalk marks as we made turns, we noticed that the backs of the buildings did not have back doors.

"I don't remember the back room of either of the storefronts I was in having a back door."

"Just when you think this place looks normal we find another little oddity that makes things seem off," Kyle stated. "Like no ventilation or the lack of sewers, or no crown in the road. Now no back doors. Strange."

"I will punch the first person who hums the *Twilight Zone* theme," Sylvia said jokingly to add some lightheartedness to the situation.

We got to the ladder. It didn't come all the way down, like a fire escape ladder, except it was not a fire escape, just a ladder that went up to the roof. There were no back windows to escape out of anyway, and it was only a one story building. The actual roof was only about twelve feet up, and the ladder came down halfway so it was easy for Larry to boost me up, which allowed me to scurry up the ladder to the flat roof. The roof itself was an old-style metal roof and seemed sturdy enough. I told everyone to come up so all of us could get some ideas from this vantage point. Larry easily boosted Kyle and Sylvia up and then grabbed the lower rung and pulled himself up with a bit of difficulty, noting that he needed to restart the regular trips to the gym to work out like he did last year.

"It's a dome! We are under a dome!" exclaimed Kyle excitedly.

From the roof we could get a better view of the layout of Oz, and indeed the biggest thing we all noticed was that the blue sky was not really a sky at all but the underside of a dome that covered the whole land of Oz. The whole dome radiated the soft blue light that replaced what would be mid-day sunlight. The light was not as monochromatic as we originally thought, it was significantly brighter in the center slowly transitioning to a dimmer and darker blue around the edges.

Looking one way we could see what looked like a central area under the middle of the dome. This was where the bigger buildings were, as well as the church with the tower. From our vantage point it looked to be about a mile away.

"I'll be anything that central area is the Town Square," Sylvia commented.

Looking the other way the single floor storefronts fanned out until the area where the dome met the ground. We could not make out exactly what was at that point as that was also about a mile or so away. If we really strained past what we assumed was the Town Square area it looked like identical storefronts went on for about two miles until the dome met the ground on that side too.

"I really wished we had some binoculars," Sylvia mused. "But I am pretty sure my parents don't have any, even if we had thought of bringing them in the first place."

On either side we could see what looked like direct, straight roads that led to the Town Square. Kyle had asked to get onto Larry's shoulders, which Larry did oblige, to get a better vantage point and do a little counting.

"Okay," Kyle said after getting down. "I think I got the layout. That center area is what we will assume for now is the Town Square. Then there are twelve straight roads that lead out from the Town Square like spokes from a bicycle wheel. This creates twelve pie shaped areas that seem to all be full of the same one-story storefronts. I think we can assume those twelve match up to the other twelve areas we can pick from on the *Oz* program. We are obviously in Greenwich and on one side is Hyde Park and the other Royal Mews. I surmise that based on the fact that they are the only other two Wi-Fi hotspots that come up on my phone. Oh, how I wish I had my directional antenna, then we could really navigate around this area. But that's back at my dorm."

"This place is huge," Sylvia said.

"I'm estimating this place to be around four miles in diameter," I added.

"And what exotic measuring device did you use to figure that out?" Kyle asked me.

"None, I'm just guessing."

"Seems about right to me," added Larry doing his own counting. "Look: there are about a dozen, no, say fifteen cross streets toward the center and the same toward the edge. While they are all different lengths due to the odd angles, they seem to average about eight storefronts each. Let's say each storefront is 25 to 30 feet wide, that's about 225 feet, add the road and you have about 250 feet, times fifteen and you end up with about three quarters a mile each way. So I think Josh is a little off, but not by too much. I say three miles in diameter."

All three of us looked at Larry in shock. He had been very quiet up to that point and then suddenly came out with this in-depth analysis.

"What? I still think this whole thing is a very bad idea, but I might as well add what I can."

"Very well done Laurence," Kyle said. "We'll make a good metrologist out of you."

"A what?"

"Metrology, Larry. It's the science of measurement."

"Oh."

"Well I have one question," Sylvia interjected. "We can see a decent amount of this place from here, but I still do not see any other people. Where is everybody?"

"What do you mean?" I asked.

"Think about it," Sylvia went on. "If this is some great new technology from Spyrius that they are working on, shouldn't we expect to see Spyrius employees inside of here doing whatever?"

"That's a really good point," I said, looking at Kyle, as we all assumed the smart one would have a logical explanation.

"I really have no idea," he answered. "But remember: when we first tried to start the *Oz* program we picked Wembley, I think, and it said it was locked and in use, or something like that. That would lead me to believe that someone else was inside. I mean, we can't see actual street level except right around us. It just seems so quiet so we assume no one else is in here, but really there could be dozens of people. Assuming a three mile diameter, this place is… umm, seven square miles."

"Yes, the area of a circle equals πr^2. We all know that one," I said.

"And of course Kyle can do that in his head," Larry said with a bit of sarcasm.

"1.5 times 1.5 equals 2.25. 2.25 times a little more than three gives us approximately seven square miles. And what are you talking about anyway Larry? You did just as complicated math in your head a second ago."

"Enough, Kyle," chided Sylvia. "Assuming we are not going to camp out on this roof, what's our next move?"

"You know," I said. "As interesting as the Town Square looks, and though it seems the logical place to go, I actually am more interested in finding out what happens in the other direction, where the dome meets the ground."

"Believe it or not, I concur," Kyle added.

"Really?" I said, which seemed too easy.

"Yes, I want to see how this place is built. The only way we are going to figure out how the outer shell meets ground level is to go there. So I'm up to going that way, mapping out as much of this place as possible and saving the central area for later."

"Unless you have any input, Larry," Sylvia said to him, "I'm following the two geniuses."

"Sounds fine to me. We should probably walk over to one of the spoke streets so it will be a straight walk though."

We all agreed and with that we climbed down from the roof and headed in the direction of one of the spoke streets. After about ten minutes of twists and turns on streets, all with the same identical storefronts, and with Sylvia duly marking with the chalk, we arrived. The main spoke street was about twice as wide as the streets we were on and it had a concrete median. The sidewalks were also wider.

"You know what this reminds me of?" asked Sylvia.

"Do tell," I said after she didn't respond to her rhetorical question.

"It reminds me of the Champs-Élysées in Paris. You know, that main tree-lined street you always see in pictures that runs to the Arc de Triomphe."

"I can see that," I said. Even though I had never been to Paris, unlike Sylvia, who has travelled all over Europe, I have seen that view in pictures and on TV plenty of times.

"You know, that brings up an interesting point that I don't think any of us have realized yet."

"What's that, Kyle?" I asked, knowing that 'I'm about to make an interesting point' look, which usually did result in some interesting point.

"There is nothing organic. No trees, no grass, no dirt, no plants in a window."

"That is an interesting point," I responded. "I guess that makes sense if this is truly an artificial world of some sort, but then there is still the point that we are organic, and obviously we are existing in this world."

Looking toward the middle we could see the Town Square in the distance, looking as quiet and desolate as the rest of the place. We turned our attention to the far edge of Oz, where the domed 'sky' met the ground and started walking, munching on some snacks along the way.

GPS did not work in Oz, but Sylvia had a pedometer program on her phone that gave an estimate of distance walked by measuring pace with the phone's gyroscopic sensor. We started the program so we would have a decent estimate of our position when we reached the end. She also stopped her video recorder. We had already been in Oz for a half hour and it didn't look like anything truly exciting was going to happen in the next fifteen minutes as we walked to the edge, so we all agreed to stop it for now. Combined with the earlier recording she estimated about an hour of recording left, so no need to waste it.

Indeed, nothing exciting happened. It took about fifteen minutes to reach the edge, and indeed it was about three quarters of a mile, according to the pedometer estimate. Along the outside edge of the dome was a street circumnavigating Oz that we could not see earlier. At least we surmised that it circumnavigated Oz based on the section we saw. Crossing that street, we walked up to where the dome wall met the ground. The dome was a shade of dark blue at this level with very little, if any, light emanating from it. There was a little curb where it met the ground, but other than that there was nothing of interest.

"Well this is a bit anticlimactic," Kyle said as he reached out to touch the wall.

"Don't touch that!" Larry yelled and Kyle froze.

"I have to agree with Larry," I said. Let's at least poke it with a pen or something just in case.

"Whatever."

So we did. We poked it with a few things. It appeared solid; no sparks came out, no demons flew down from the sky. Kyle finally reached out and pressed his hand against the wall and nothing happened.

"See," he said with a bit of contempt in his voice.

"Don't be sarcastic," I chided him a little. "We're making group decisions here and it doesn't hurt to be a little careful, you know."

Kyle apologized, seemingly sincere, but he was right: the dome wall was pretty ordinary. It seemed to be made of a Plexiglas-type material, hard and strong, but with a slight transparency that would allow light to go through. There was no way of determining how thick it was or what possibly could be on the other side, if anything.

"So we walked all the way to the end here and it seems to be a bust," Sylvia stated.

"Maybe, maybe not," Kyle responded. "I mean, yeah, it doesn't seem like we are finding anything interesting here that would tell us more about what Oz is or how it works or why it even exists, but if we didn't come all the way down here we would never have known. So we still gained needed knowledge, even though it doesn't seem very useful."

"Very pragmatic of you."

"Just trying to take a methodical and objective approach to analyzing this place, Sylvia. So I guess our next move is to go to the Town Square."

Sylvia, Larry and I shared the same knowing glance. It was 9:00 pm at this point and we had a pretty eventful day. I felt it would be a good idea to go back to the portal now, even if we were planning to go to the Town Square, just to be on the safe side and make sure everything was still as we left it. If I felt that way, I knew Sylvia, and most definitely Larry did as well. It would be another twenty minutes at least to get back to the portal, and checking things out would take us to 9:30. I was thinking we should call it a night and start fresh the next day, but I also knew, all three of us knew, that Kyle was not going to take that well. Sylvia took it upon herself to broach the subject.

"I was thinking, Kyle, that we should head back to the portal, make sure everything is okay and then maybe say that might be enough exploring for today."

"I concur," I immediately added before Kyle could put up any objection. "Look Kyle, I can tell you just want to run around here all night, but it's been a long day and we have all day tomorrow to explore. Remember we are only an hour from school so we don't have to leave to get back until night."

"But," was all I would let Kyle get out. From his look I wasn't sure if he was about to cry, throw a fit, or become defiant. Regardless I was going to try to answer every objection he would have before he could come up with it. I have long since found that was the best way to deal with Kyle when you wanted to do something different than what he was planning.

"Look, we have it running through the anonymous proxy. No one's going to come in the middle of the night and take it. We've done enough that even if for some really weird reason Spyrius shut this whole thing down I am sure we could get an audience with them."

"We need to get back to the portal now and make sure we can get back to Sylvia's."

That was Larry, and he said it pretty definitively. He was going along with things okay at first, but I could tell he was reaching his breaking point and wanted to get back to familiar territory. The last thing he was going to stand for was getting into a debate with Kyle. Unlike Sylvia and I, who don't mind Kyle's sometimes annoying personality, Larry has issues when Kyle is at his most bothersome. Kyle does not help matters by being very bad at picking up the subtle cues when Larry is getting irked. Larry tolerates it most times, but now, when he was in a situation he didn't really want to be in, he was not going to tolerate anything. I didn't want to see this escalate because it would not be pretty.

I stopped reasoning with Kyle, walked over to him and moved him a bit away from Sylvia and Larry.

"Don't say a word. Not now. We are going back through the portal to Sylvia's and you can argue with me then. But not now."

I do give Kyle credit for some things. He usually is pretty good at listening to me when I am really decisive in telling him what to do, especially in social situations, even if he doesn't agree or quite understand the reasons. Maybe it's a bit of the big brother/little brother part of our relationship or maybe he just simply trusts me enough, but fortunately he took my advice.

"Fine," he said under his breath, clearly not happy that he was not given the chance to even argue his point, let alone get his way.

We walked back following the way we came, turning right into the Greenwich area when we got to the chalk marks that Sylvia had drawn. We followed the marks left and right back to the storefront where the purple portal lied. We had no issues. Kyle was obviously not happy, but I kept him right next to me, behind Larry and Sylvia so Larry would not pick up on Kyle's attitude.

Back in the storefront nothing had changed. I told everyone to hold on a second and I stuck my head through real quick just to make sure Sylvia's laundry room was on the other end. It was.

"You know," I said right before we went back through the portal. "It's almost as odd that absolutely nothing at all has happened the whole time we've been in here."

Sylvia shook her head in agreement. Kyle was too bummed to care and Larry just wanted to get back. With that we all went through the portal and came out in Sylvia's laundry room just like we left it.

Chapter 7

I went to shut down the portal. Sylvia was keenly aware that she should get Larry away from Kyle, who was going to need to vent before he lost his temper.

"Larry, why don't you give me a hand? I need to get some blankets and pillows set up for the guest bedroom." Turning to Kyle and me, she added, "There's only a single bed so I hope you don't mind sharing. It's a queen though, so I think you will be okay." Then she left with Larry in tow.

Kyle quietly shut the door.

"Why are you shutting it down, aren't we going back in?"

Maybe Kyle was hoping I was just going along with Sylvia and Larry until we got back and then would side with him and go back in, or maybe he thought he could sway me when it was just him and me, but either way I had a long day and didn't want a fight. Unfortunately it looked like I was not being given a choice.

"What part of 'wait until tomorrow' did you not understand?" I said, far too abruptly than I probably should have.

"Well, find then. You three can go downstairs and watch some stupid sitcom, but I plan on going back in."

"No."

"And just what gives you the right to tell me what I can or cannot do? Contrary to what you might think, you are not my keeper."

"No I am not. But neither is this your toy to play with as you see fit. We found this as a group and we are going to make decisions on its use as a group."

"Oh yeah, 'as a group.' Just like getting the apartment, that's code for 'the three of us decide and Kyle doesn't have a damn bit of input.' This is the greatest event that's ever happened in my menial life and you just want me - no you are telling me - I have to abandon it just because some of you are tired? Well screw you, Josh, you don't have that right."

I knew Kyle wanted a fight. Heck, he relished a fight. I often think that his maturity is inversely proportional with his intelligence. He knew full well that the decision was made, and though he was right about us making the decision without any input from him, it was because we already knew his position. He would argue for the rest of the night if he felt that's what it would take for all of us to know how unfair we were being to him. Sometimes I didn't mind getting into a good row with him, but not this time, so I figured I would try to take another tactic entirely.

"Look, Kyle," I said in a purposely soft tone, as I sat down on the floor and looked up at him. "I know you probably don't believe it, but I am just an intrigued, excited and anxious to go back and explore as you are. However I think it's wise to take the night to process everything that has happened so far and figure out a plan for how to proceed. Look, you and I are in charge here and instead of arguing till the cows come home, I would much rather spend the next hour or so until we call it a night comparing notes, coming up with ideas and theories and figuring out a plan together. Though you may think it utterly stupid, I don't think it's wise for you to go in there alone. There are too many unknowns about whatever Oz is. You are my best friend and I don't want anything to happen to you."

I think Kyle was probably more annoyed that I didn't let him finish venting than not being able to go back into Oz.

"But what if it's not there tomorrow?!" he pleaded.

"Want to know the single biggest concern I have had this whole time? Which I obviously could not say in front of Larry for fear of spooking him?"

"What?"

"What if we are in there and the plug is pulled? If Oz is some sort of technology like we think it is, then that means it can be shut down at any time. What if it gets shut down while we are in it? Would we nicely appear back here, or…? The point is, if it's still there tomorrow morning, lasting through the whole night, then I will have a much greater confidence that it has a permanence that will allow us to explore to our heart's content."

"And if it's not?"

"Well, to be honest if it's not then I am damn well happy that we got out safe and sound when we did."

"But…"

"Look, I know you are aching to explore, but even if it's not there tomorrow for whatever reason, we've been in it. We know what is. I don't know what our next move will be if it's not. Contact Spyrius, I guess. I mean, we wouldn't go 'public' with this, no one would believe us. Plus I'm assuming Spyrius wants to keep this internal, for now at least. The point is we know and have experienced whatever this is, and that can never be taken away."

I could see the wheels turning in Kyle's brain as he tried to figure out some angle he could exploit in my logic, but ultimately he could not come up with one.

"Okay," he said with a sigh, but a smile on his face. "But I just want to it noted that I will officially be upset if it is not there tomorrow morning."

"Duly noted!"

As we walked away he asked if I was going to take that laptop and put it somewhere so he could not sneak off in the middle of the night and go into Oz. I told him no and that I trusted him, which I figured would actually made him less likely to do anything sneaky. And so, with that drama taken care of, we went downstairs.

We all got some snacks and then Sylvia and Larry retreated up to Sylvia's room, leaving Kyle and me in the family room. With the TV on in the background, we discussed everything that happened that day, throwing around ideas and hypotheses on the nature of Oz and considering plans for what to do next. Ultimately we didn't come up with anything new or groundbreaking. As for a plan of action we agreed that going to the Town Square was the next logical move, but we really couldn't come up with what to do after that. We would play it by ear and see what the Town Square held and then take it from there. I think we were both a little worried that the Town Square would hold nothing different or interesting from what we had already seen. With such amazing technology we were expecting something amazing to happen when used, but, to be honest, our exploring so far in this land of Oz, had been a bit, well, uninspiring.

At about 11:00 pm we retreated up to the guest bedroom. The queen-size bed was plenty big enough for both of to not feel weird. I had bunk beds when Kyle and I first met as 13-year-old high-school freshmen. As a little kid I loved the bunk beds, but as a newly minted teenager I was going to get rid of them and get a real bed, but fairly quickly in our friendship Kyle started staying over a lot. I think because his family life was very cold, unemotional and boring he really relished staying at my place. Partially for hanging out with me, but just as much to be part of the more normal family atmosphere. So I kept the bunk beds (though I did get a new, more comfortable and more adult mattress, and moved from the top to the bottom bunk). Oddly, except for one night when my parents and sister went out of town, I never stayed over at Kyle's.

"You know the one thing I really wonder about?" I said as we lay in bed waiting for the fog of sleep to seep into our brains.

"What's that?" Kyle mumbled.

"Considering how secret this must be to Spyrius, it's odd that we are able to run rampant in it. I would think they would have some monitoring system that sends alerts when people are inside. After all, we *are* connected to Spyrius while this is running. You would think they wouldn't want some unknown college kids learning about it."

"Don't know. Have some ideas, but it's all total conjecture. We should try to get to sleep; I want to get up early."

I think we both stayed awake for a while. Just too much excitement to fall asleep immediately. But we both kept quiet and after a while I finally fell off to a deep slumber.

I awoke the next morning lying on my side. Kyle was lying on his back with his eyes open. My left arm was resting across Kyle, and I quickly pulled it away, slightly embarrassed.

"I was going to give you five more minutes before waking you up. I want to know if you had your arm around me on purpose so you would notice if I tried to get up and go to Oz, or if that was subconscious."

"I didn't have my arm around you. It was lying on you. And no, in either case. What time is it anyway?"

"Eight-thirty in the morning."

I sighed. I could have easily slept another hour, but I knew there was no way that Kyle was going to allow that. It would be like telling a five-year-old to be patient on Christmas morning.

"Okay, but you have to have a certain amount of patience. We need to get Larry and Sylvia up, eat breakfast and I, for one, want a shower. So, patience, Kyle, patience…"

We got up and Sylvia and Larry emerged from their lair, aka Sylvia's bedroom. Larry went downstairs to see what was available for breakfast. Since Sylvia's parents had left for an extended vacation the pickings were pretty thin, but Larry found some bacon and hash browns in the freezer. Larry was a decent cook so he took it upon himself to start making a big pile of bacon and potato hash for breakfast.

"Larry and I came to a decision on what we want to do," Sylvia announced to us. "We are going to go in and join you on a trek to the Town Square area to see what is there. But assuming it's not much different from what we have already seen, we will come back and that will be it for us. After that what you two want to do with this thing is up to you."

Kyle and I looked at each other. We had no idea what their attitude would be this morning: if they would want to join us to the Town Square or even if the two of them would be on the same page. So, Sylvia's proclamation was great as far as we were concerned.

"Fantastic," I said. "That is just what we were wanting to do."

"But first," Sylvia said, looking straight at Kyle, "I want to eat, take a shower and get ready. Don't rush us."

"No fear, Sylvia," I responded. "Already been over that."

"Fine," Kyle said, genuinely okay with it. "But while Larry is cooking breakfast I want to at least boot up the program and stick our heads through to make sure everything is still the same."

Sylvia and Larry agreed and Kyle and I went upstairs to start the program. We picked Greenwich again, the portal came up, we stuck our heads through and everything looked exactly the same as the day before.

"Feel better now?" I asked.

"Much," Kyle said, looking around as if he was trying to see if anyone was spying on him. "Real quick, let's pick another place. I just want to look through for a second."

"I think we should stick with Greenwich for now. We can try a different entrance after we do the Town Square excursion."

"Fine, fine, no issues, not going to argue. Just want to try another real quick just to see."

I could see the pleading in him. The kind of look that said 'let me have this one little thing, I don't want to argue but I might'. And frankly, I was interested too.

"Okay, quickly though. What do you want to pick?"

"What do you think?"

I pressed option 13 for the Kelvedon Hatch Nuclear Bunker. I guess we both figured that if any place would have something different from what we already saw it would be the one with the weirdest name. We were wrong. Sticking our heads through we saw the same storefront type building we saw in Greenwich. The colors were slightly different, the wood a slightly different shade, but otherwise everything was exactly the same both in the building and the street outside.

"Well that's disappointing," Kyle noted.

"We better get back before Sylvia and Larry wonder what we are up to. Plus I am hungry and that bacon smells good."

Breakfast was indeed very good and we all ate until we were stuffed.

Before leaving our apartment at Tech, Larry and I packed a change of clothes and a toothbrush. Sylvia obviously had what she needed here. Since we didn't stop at Kyle's dorm I brought a clean shirt of mine for him as we wear the same size. He would just have to survive for a day without clean underwear. We all took quick showers and packed up the backpacks with the same things as yesterday, adding some Granola bars and Pop Tarts Sylvia had to replace the snacks we ate yesterday. Sylvia's camera was all recharged and ready to go. It was about 9:45 am when we were all upstairs in the laundry room ready to embark on another journey into Oz.

All four of us went through the portal at Greenwich with no issues. We took a look around the storefront, but nothing had changed. Outside everything looked the same as yesterday; even Sylvia's chalk markings were still there. It was like no time had passed at all since we were last here the day before. Facing toward the center of the Town Square area, we decided to go toward the spoke road between Greenwich and what we assumed was Royal Mews instead of the road between Greenwich and Hyde Park that we had taken yesterday, just to see if there was any difference. After a few twists and turns, with Sylvia marking the path in a new color, we arrived at the spoke road. There were no major differences in taking our new route, just endless rows of identical storefronts like before. Kyle verified with his phone that we were picking up Wi-Fi signals from both Greenwich and Royal Mews. We could see the Town Square in the distance, which we assumed was about three quarters of a mile away based on our estimates from the day before. We started walking toward it.

As we got closer we could start to make out exactly what the Town Square was, slowly perceiving more and more as we got closer. The Town Square was not square at all, but circular in nature and probably about a quarter mile in diameter. The dozen spoke roads radiated out from the Town Square, forming the twelve pie shaped sections. Town Square was just a big open space except for an old sixteenth century looking church, complete with bell tower, right in the middle. Each of the twelve areas that terminated at Town Square had a four-story brick office building facing into the square. Looking toward the square we could see all the identical one-story storefronts go up to the back of the four-story office building.

Larry was busy sketching the scene as we entered the square. Up to this point Larry had been fairly quiet but pretty content, a minor but distinct contrast to the anxious silence he displayed the day before. I really hadn't talked to Larry much about how he was feeling, as I felt that Sylvia was taking care of that and I didn't want to say the wrong thing. I think maybe Sylvia had suggested he sketch things along the way so he would have some busy work to do. While Larry finished his sketch we all stood around in the square, taking in the architecture that was finally different from the endless storefronts. Sylvia was panning her video camera around to get a 360 degree view while Kyle was using his phone to take some pictures. Soon Larry finished his sketch and showed it to me.

"Not bad," I said. "You did a great job of capturing an overhead view of where we are from your vantage point here on the ground."

Actually it wasn't that great at all, and the scale was off, but if it kept Larry happy and occupied then I was only going to be encouraging.

The circular square itself looked like something straight out of any European city. The actual street was made from cobblestone giving a distinctly old world feel which also blended with the stone church in the middle. The church itself was rectangular, complete with an iron door, stained glass, flying buttresses and gargoyles. The square itself was pretty barren except for four freestanding rectangular stone walls about three feet high, eight feet wide and three feet deep near each corner of the church. By those walls were some wrought iron tables and chairs, a few wooden benches and some carts, like the ones flower salesmen would use. However there were no flowers, and like the rest of Oz there were no trees, no grass or any other organic matter.

"It's so odd," I pointed out to no one in particular. "The storefronts look like something from the American Old West, except for the metal shelves in the back. The roads look like modern asphalt, those brick office buildings look early twentieth century and the actual square and church look like something out of sixteenth century Europe. Very odd combination."

"This is definitely Town Square," Kyle said, done taking his pictures. "The only Wi-Fi signal I am picking up right now is labeled as such. I will bet anything that the hot spot and any portal are inside the church. We should go inside."

At this point I had migrated over to Kyle who was standing near one of the flower carts. Sylvia, had put her camera back on her head strap and walked over to Larry, who was standing by one of those little walls, to see his drawing. I was just gazing at the church in general and Kyle had his nose in his phone. Then I noticed, for the first time since we entered Oz, we weren't alone.

Chapter 8

I am still not sure if I saw the movement first or heard the voices first, but regardless I became aware of a group of people coming out of one of the spoke streets onto the square in front and to the right of us. They were heading toward us. I quickly grabbed Kyle and told him to get down behind the flower cart. Across from us I could see Sylvia and Larry getting down behind the wall. I am not sure if they noticed the group at the same time or if they were just following my lead, but I waived to them to stay down.

"What's going on?" Kyle asked.

"Quiet," I said in a whisper. "There are people coming our way."

Sylvia and Larry were well covered behind the wall. Kyle and I were barely hidden behind the flower cart. In fact someone looking straight at the cart would be able to see our legs behind the large back wheels.

"Why are we hiding?" Kyle whispered back to me. "Why don't we go greet them?"

"For starters we are probably not supposed to be here, and second, something does not feel right."

I could not put my finger on it, but something just felt wrong with the group that was approaching. They were still too far away to comprehend what they were saying but I definitely could make out the people's faces from looking through the slats in the top of the flower cart.

They were a group of five. One man, a tall, fairly stocky middle-aged white man with slightly greying hair, seemed to be the ringleader. He was doing most of the talking and was pointing out different things. He was dressed casually and seemed like he knew what Oz was about so I assumed he was from Spyrius. There were two other people that also seemed to be Spyrius employees as both were wearing the red Spyrius shirts. One looked younger, Asian, and just had the air of being a technical person. The fact that he had a Spyrius touchscreen laptop in tablet mode, with two decent sized antennas clipped on, gave credence to that theory. The other man was large, muscular and maybe Caribbean but most definitely in shape.

The other two looked foreign. Not just in their cultural makeup, though they did look Indian or Middle Eastern, but foreign in the fact that they were both wearing expensive suits and seemed to be getting a tour of Oz from the ringleader and the other two. Those two just looked very out of place, and that probably added to my concern.

Kyle held his phone close to the ground under the cart and took some pictures. I was not happy that he was doing this but at that point I couldn't say anything because the group was getting close enough where we could now make out what they were saying. Fortunately they did not seem to notice us.

"...much more diversity... brick buildings here were the second stab. Obviously the church here is the coup de grâce so far. Though as you noticed the inside still has a lot of work to be done. Let's go sit at that table over there and we can discuss what you have seen."

This was coming from the ringleader as he led the group to one of the wrought iron tables. They pulled up five chairs, stealing one from a nearby table, and all sat down. The table was next to the wall that Sylvia and Larry were behind, so while they could not see a thing they could hear everything loud a clear. Kyle and I were probably about fifty feet away, behind the cart, which was turned about a thirty degrees toward the group, with myself being closer to them and Kyle to my right. The good thing was that not only could we hear the group just fine, we could see them pretty easily. The bad thing was that we were not well hidden at all. While they did not seem concerned about anyone eavesdropping I knew all it would take was one wrong move by either Kyle or me and we would be exposed.

I could just barely see Sylvia from our angle. Larry was to her left so I could not really see him, but I knew he was there. Sylvia was looking at us, as she had nothing better to look at. I was really hoping she was still recording so we could get to the audio. I carefully pointed to my head where she had the camera and she shook her head in the affirmative.

"It seems so quiet in this place," one of the foreign men in the suits noted. "Is there no one else in here?"

"No," said the ringleader. "Not much work goes on during the weekend. That's why I picked seven o'clock on a Sunday morning for this. Remember there are only about fifteen or twenty people who even have access to this."

I thought the time was odd. It was about half past ten at this point, had they really been in this place for over three hours?

"I noticed before we came in that Kyle and his architect wife had signed up to go in this morning," said the technical guy.

"What?" said the ringleader, turning to the technical guy, looking less than happy and then lowering his voice such that we couldn't pick up everything, "Didn't... tell..."

"They're over... House. And... edge ...nowhere near us," said the technical guy.

"Is there a problem?" Foreign man number two asked.

"No, none at all. There might be two others in here, but they're in the Yorke House section over there," the ringleader said while point over his shoulder to the left. "They are working on creating a new building against the far wall so they are at least a mile away from us. It will be no issue at all."

"Let me recap this," Foreign man number one stated. "I am seeing two big possibilities. One is to put a door behind the enemy and then funnel an unlimited amount of people though."

"Yes, that is correct, though we still have some testing to do."

"And you will let us know immediately of the results."

"Of course."

"The second is a place to hide, or make disappear, people."

"Yes, of course, though there are many other ways in which this can be used."

"I understand, but I need to take back to my client the most useful possibilities for them. You are asking for a bid of a considerable amount of money."

"Understood."

"Now, you said this will be available to the winning bidder only. How can I be sure you will not share this technology with others?"

"You can't. But that is part of why you are paying so much. For exclusivity. We anticipate a bid of such value that we would have no reason not to be exclusive. Remember that although you are the first we still have others to show this to, so please bid well."

"What about Lord Danbridge and the, what did you say, fifteen to twenty others that know of this?"

"Like you said: this can be used to make people, well, disappear. I am fully trusted by the Lordship himself. I will have no problem cleaning everything up so you will be the only ones with this technology. Lord

Danbridge already has a reputation as an eccentric. Just vanishing off the face of the Earth will only add to his lore."

With that Kyle poked me. Obviously I understood what the ringleader was doing. Sylvia got it too as I could see the surprise in her face. Unfortunately Kyle's little poke made just enough noise to catch the technical guy's attention. He looked up and then straight at us.

"What the!" he exclaimed loudly.

We were busted.

"Somebody's there, behind the cart," he said.

The ringleader turned, looked puzzled for a second, but then noticed us too.

"Get them, Bradley," He said to the large muscular guy as everyone stood up.

"Run," I said to Kyle. No prompting was needed as he was already taking his first step. We started running away from them, which was also away from Sylvia and Larry and away from the Greenwich area that we came from. Not that we had any choice.

"Who the hell? Kill them if you need!" the ringleader exclaimed.

"I'm not sure if you can shoot them," technical guy said.

With that I looked back to see that Bradley, the big one, had what looked like a very real gun. While Kyle and I had youth, Bradly was obviously in shape and gaining on us.

"Bradley STOP!" technical guy yelled at the top of his lungs. "You're almost out of range. We'll be exposed."

Bradley stopped, we didn't.

"Everyone move! Now! Run!" the ringleader commanded. "Stay near Cho, but move it. We need to get those two!"

Now they were a group of five pursuing us, and for whatever reason they needed to stay near Cho, the technical guy, or more probably his laptop. This now gave us the upper hand. I started running toward the nearest spoke street but I noticed Kyle look back, count off something with his fingers, and then turn to the left.

"Follow me!" he urged.

He was veering off to the left, heading toward another street. This seemed to extend the time before we could lose our pursuers in the side streets but I was smart enough to realize that Kyle seemed to have a plan or some sort. Since I had absolutely no plan at all I could see no reason to debate his request, so I followed him.

"We're losing them," ringleader said. "Track them Cho."

"I can't, it will blow… cover program."

"Damn…"

By the time Kyle and I reached the spoke street he wanted we had put quite a bit of distance between us and the group chasing us. We could no longer make out what they were saying. Kyle actually slowed down a bit.

"What are you doing?" I asked Kyle. Though frankly I was out of breath.

"We need to make sure they keep following us so Larry and Sylvia can get away and get back to the Greenwich portal, assuming they have enough sense to do that!"

"Where are we going?"

"Yorke House portal. It's number one on that list of the sections in Oz, this one right here," Kyle said as he pointed to the storefronts to the left of us.

"You remember that?" I asked almost rhetorically as I knew Kyle had an almost photographic memory. "But why?"

"That guy said two people came in at Yorke House. So there should be an active portal there."

"And if not?"

"Then we're screwed. Come on."

With that we could hear the group getting closer and about to round the corner to the main street. We hightailed it down the street as fast as we could, covering a half a mile in about three and a half minutes. The group was following us down the street for a while but stopped when they realized they were not going to catch us. I had no idea what they were planning on doing next but I had no time to figure it out because at the next intersection Kyle called out, "turn left here!"

And we did. By that point we were out of breath and just jogging. I followed Kyle through lefts and rights and rights and lefts again through endless storefronts for about five or six minutes until Kyle stopped.

"Here it is. Damn, I am good!"

"Normally, Kyle I would chide you for being so cocky and arrogant, but not today."

Indeed, right in front of us was a storefront with a very inviting, slightly shimmering purple portal inside.

"I surmised that all of the twelve pie shaped sections are exactly the same," Kyle said as we walked inside. "So I just followed the route from yesterday."

"Which you of course had memorized."

"How long have you known me?"

"Not complaining, except that I guess we didn't need Sylvia's chalk after all."

"Probably was still a good idea."

We both stared at the portal for a moment as if we weren't sure what the best course of action was. I figured Kyle was doing pretty well so far, so I asked him.

"What shall we do?"

"I guess we need to go through. I'm sure those guys realized this is where we were going. Once we are though we can pull the plug."

"They seemed to stop back there."

"Yeah, but we can't count on that. I think this is a better bet than going back to Greenwich. In fact I really hope Larry and Sylvia got back, went through and shut it down."

"What about the other two people that came in through here. Some guy named Kyle and his architect wife?"

"I think they're fine, Josh. I mean that group obviously wanted to stay unknown, so they are not going to announce themselves to those two."

"But wouldn't they be stuck in here if we shut it down?"

"I guarantee Spyrius has some way of getting them out. Two things that Cho guy said make me think that. First, they signed up to go in, so people know they are here. Second, the fact that he told that big guy to stop because it would blow their cover program leads me to believe everything in here is tracked and they had to do something special to hide themselves."

"Then why are they letting us run rampant if they know we are in here?"

"Uh, okay so I don't have an answer for that one. But we need to go through now if we are going to go through."

"Let's make sure it's safe first."

"Okay." Kyle stuck his hand through the portal and then pulled it back out.

"That's not what I… Wait!" I tried to say to Kyle but with his hand coming back intact of he proceeded to stick his head in. Fortunately it too came back fine.

"One of these days you're going to really…"

"It's safe, let's go," he said as he went through.

It is safe, but are we safe? I wondered to myself. I had no real option but to follow.

We entered a den or possibly the library of a house. Whatever it was, there were a lot of books about and the place was very messy. Not dirty messy, but messy as in papers and boxes lying around, as well as a smattering of other stuff strewn about the place. There wasn't much time for sightseeing; we needed to shut the portal down.

"I'll just pull the plug," I said to Kyle.

"No, wait," he said as he went behind the projector to the computer controlling it, a Spyrius laptop not unlike mine. "There is no screensaver. It's booted straight to the command prompt. I can just shut it down."

Unlike what I did where my laptop was in the graphic interface with the program running under a non-graphic command prompt, this laptop was booted straight into the command line interface. And while you can still have a locking screensaver on the command line, in this case whoever was running it did not.

"Hit 'Q' to quit and 'Y' to confirm," I said and Kyle did.

Checking Door
Oz Clear
Closing Door

The projector shut off and the purple door disappeared just as ours had.

"I wonder…" Kyle said to himself as he typed a few commands into the laptop. "Yep, he has nothing running. I mean nothing but the absolute bare minimum plus basic networking. I wonder if you're supposed to run this straight from the command prompt with nothing unnecessary running."

"Probably to lessen the chance of a crash?" I hypothesized. "Even though Spyrius machines are almost totally crash proof."

"Almost totally does not mean totally crash proof."

"Oops. Well, umm, too late now! I'm unplugging the projector anyway, just in case you can remotely activate it somehow."

Just then my phone vibrated. It was my missed text nag. I had a missed call and a text from Sylvia. I pulled the plug from the projector first and was going to call her back when she beat me to the punch and called again.

"Joe's Pizza," I answered. I don't know, that's more like something Kyle would do, but I needed a little levity.

"What the? Josh? You asshole! Are you okay? Is Kyle okay? Where are you? I've been trying to call you."

"We're both okay, don't worry. Though I have no idea where we are."

I caught Sylvia up to speed on what happened to us. Sylvia and Larry did what we had hoped they would do, hightailing it back to the portal in Greenwich once our pursuers were out of view and ending up back at Sylvia's house. Larry, who was never really comfortable with any of this, wanted to pull the plug on the projector just in case any of the bad guys came through. Sylvia insisted that they had to keep it open until they heard from us. According to Sylvia it was getting very heated between her and Larry, and when they knew we were safe Larry finally lost it. I could hear his outburst hear though the phone.

"*They're safe?*"

"Yes, both of them."

"*Where are they?*"

"I don't know."

"*But they are in the real world, right?*"

"Yes, I guess."

"*In that case that is it. This damn thing is never being used again.*"

"What are you doing?!"

I then heard the smashing of glass and a lot of yelling between Sylvia and Larry. Kyle was looking at me with an inquisitive look, but I could only tell him to hold on. Finally Sylvia seemed to move into another room and obviously Larry went somewhere else as I could not hear him anymore. Sylvia was almost in tears.

"He smashed the projector. I've never seen him this mad. He's totally lost it."

"Smashed the projector?" I said.

"Yes, he ripped the cord out then took a hammer from over the washing machine and smashed the lens of the projector. It's not going to work now. He's going on about how he never wanted to go in, how stupid we were, saying it's all Kyle's fault, though why it's his fault I don't know."

"What do you mean smashed the projector?" Kyle asked me.

"Hold on, Kyle. Sylvia, don't worry about it. We're safe."

"Does Sylvia have the camera? Did she record everything?"

"What, Kyle?"

"The camera, the camera. Did Sylvia record everything those people said?"

"I don't know, Sylvia, Kyle wants to know if you recorded everything they said on the camera."

"Yes I did," Sylvia responded to me, but still quite upset. "But it fell off my head when we were running. It's somewhere on the side streets in that Greenwich area. I'm sorry Josh, but I can't deal with that now."

"Well does she have it?"

"Kyle, calm down. Sylvia is very upset and Larry's gone off the deep end."

"This is extremely important. I just need to know if she recorded everything and has the camera."

"Yes. I mean, no. I mean, she recorded it, but they lost the camera running on the side streets of Greenwich."

"Lost it!" With that Kyle put his hands on his head and just shook his head back and forth. I'm not sure why he was so upset, but I had to deal with Sylvia.

"I'm sorry Josh," Sylvia said again, obviously overhearing Kyle's reaction. "You two are fully safe now, right?"

"Yes, we are safe."

"Then I got to go. I'll call you back later, okay?"

"Okay," I said. "It will be fine, relax, everyone is okay. I'll talk to you soon."

I hung up with Sylvia. I sat down and took a deep breath. Kyle lifted his hands up from his head and looked at me.

"We have to go back in and get that camera."

Chapter 9

"Think about it Josh," Kyle said to me. "That group is ready to sell this technology to the highest bidder and then kill Lord Danbridge and everyone else at Spyrius who knows about this. Obviously the ringleader is someone who Lord Danbridge trusts so we need to get that camera and then we need to get to Lord Danbridge so we can prove to him what is going on. And let me tell you, I am sure those people in the suits are not planning to use this technology to further world peace. Not only that, holy…!"

"What?"

"Look at that clock. Look what time it is, do you know where we are?" he said as was looking at his phone, presumably at the mapping program.

"Obviously I don't."

Kyle pulled aside the drapes and peaked out of the window. "Yep, it's barely past eight in the morning. We're at Harvey Mudd College!"

I stared at Kyle. He obviously had some odd assumption that Harvey Mudd College was supposed to mean something to me. But what was obvious when I looked at the time on my phone, which automatically changes time across time zones, was that we were now in the Pacific Time Zone, three hours behind Eastern. We didn't enter Oz until almost 10:00 am and now it should be 11:00 in the morning, but instead the phone clock was showing 8:00 am.

"Harvey Mudd. It's a genius technical school on par with MIT or Carnegie Mellon, but much smaller. Kind of have to be in the know. Lord Danbridge went to school here. Heck, I was accepted there and I told you. Obviously you weren't paying attention."

"That's because all you kept telling me was that you wanted to go to Tech with me."

"Yeah. Whatever. Remember Debbie Engles?"

"The one on your debate team who only missed one question on the SATs, but was overshadowed because you got a perfect score?"

"Yeah, her. I don't think she really liked me. Anyway, she goes here."

"Great, but you still haven't told me where here is."

"Los Angeles. As in California. As in 3,000 miles away from where we started."

I checked the mapping program on my phone. He was right: we were in Los Angeles, California. Actually, technically we were in Claremont, about thirty miles east of Los Angeles in a subdivision right across the street from the Claremont Colleges, of which Harvey Mudd was one of five schools that shared the same campus. One look outside the window at the trees and architecture of the house across from us verified that we were not in Virginia anymore. This also explained why the ringleader said seven o'clock. They must have entered Oz from a portal on the west coast.

"This is incredible Josh. You know what this means?"

"Well, uh, pretty obvious. It means we traveled 3,000 miles in mere seconds."

"This means Oz can be used as a teleporter. That's what that guy in the suit meant when he said that you can funnel an unlimited amount of people behind an enemy. Could you imagine if a terrorist snuck a single projector into a military base, or Government building, or something like the Freedom Tower? They could funnel in hundreds of people with guns, bombs, anything. That could be really bad."

"Okay, I am not disagreeing, but we can't go back in right now. I don't think those people can do anything yet. Remember they said that the suits were only the first people they had shown the technology to, and that there was still testing to be done."

"True, but I wonder if our appearance might have changed their plans."

"Maybe, but they just can't eliminate everyone now if there is still work to be done before they can sell it."

"Okay, let me think for a second." With Kyle, that really meant about a second. "I agree, we have some time and we can't risk going back in right now. We will also assume that the bad guys know nothing of Larry and Sylvia and the camera. Let's look around here. I want to use a computer with a full sized monitor, if we can find one, to see if I can figure out who that one guy is from the pictures I took with my phone. My smartphone screen just won't cut it, the picture's way too small."

"The ringleader?"

"Yeah, if he's really close to Lord Danbridge we will be able to find something on him."

"I think we can assume the people that live here are the other Kyle guy and his architect wife that are working in Oz. Look: there are pictures of a couple and some architectural house models here."

"Even if they come back, I think they are good guys. They might even be able to help us, if we can get them to believe us."

So we went to explore the house we were in. It was a fairly small single family home probably built in the 1950s, when a small, 1,000 square foot house was normal, and it was still mostly original. The front door opened to a living room, dining room, and kitchen area (though the dining room was tiny). The portal was in a separate library, or den, where there looked to be a newly installed dryer plug for the projector.

Down a hall there were three bedrooms and a single bathroom. Attached to the house was a one car garage full of car batteries arranged in parallel and tied to the house electrical panel. We came to the conclusion that this probably served as a hot backup to keep the projector running in case of a power outage while in Oz.

"Probably a good idea," I said. "And not something Sylvia's house has."

"Too late to worry about that," Kyle replied.

Looking out the windows, discretely so no neighbors saw us, you can see that the neighborhood was a mix of a few original houses, but a lot of teardowns and rebuilds from various eras. Normally I think I would have felt it very weird and very wrong to be trespassing in a total stranger's house like this, but after everything we have been though with Oz in the past day it somehow seemed okay. Almost normal.

A little digging gave us all the information on the occupants we needed. Kyle and Sarah Vaughn were married, probably in their early thirties and seemed to have no children. Kyle taught computer science full-time at Harvey Mudd while Sarah appeared to be an architect, though we couldn't tell if she worked for a firm or was freelance. It also seemed that she taught at least one course in architecture at Pitzer College, one of the other Claremont colleges. How they got hooked up with Spyrius Corporation we did not know, but they were obviously doing side work on the *Oz* project for Spyrius.

In a spare bedroom turned Sarah's office, we found a nice, regular Windows desktop computer that we thought we could use. Though it had a password protected screensaver.

"Didn't think it would be that easy," I said. "There is a computer science professor living here."

"Too bad this isn't the movies or one of those TV shows, then we would just be able to magically guess the password. Or better yet, we could just summon some unearthly force, type a few keystrokes, watch some random stuff fly across the screen and then suddenly exclaim, 'I'm in!' with no rhyme or reason."

"A lot of people do have really bad passwords," I pointed out.

"Okay, I'll try 'password', nope. '12345678', nope. 'querty', nope. Well, I don't think I would want to be working within her login anyway. That's why I keep several portable, bootable operating systems on this keychain USB drive at all times. This way I can just boot up my own instance and not have to worry about getting into her machine. After all, I just want to surf the web."

I've always gotten a kick out of watching a TV show that has anything to do with hacking or computer technology with Kyle and his dad. The two of them go crazy when characters break into agency systems with NSA-level security and then bypass all security measures effortlessly. They are both incapable of suspending belief and enjoying a fictional show for what it is.

"Looks like I have to go into the BIOS to set allowing boot from USB," Kyle said. After a bit, "Okay, I am logged into my own instance. Their Wi-Fi uses WEP, but I can tether my phone, this has Bluetooth. Okay, transferred that picture I took. Let's search here. Hmm… Oh, wow. He's Randy Hanson, Directory of Security for Spyrius and childhood friend of Lord Danbridge."

"How did you find that out so fast?" I asked.

"Well, Josh, I just Googled 'pictures of Spyrius executives' and came up with a nice list. Google: it's this little search tool, you *might* have heard of it. Though it is pretty obscure."

I felt like punching Kyle for that snide remark, but then again I walked into that one. Kyle is so good at computer exploits that I often assume anything he does is some incredible feat of hacking. In reality, his methods are usually simpler than I imagine.

He waited a moment to see if I was going to hit him, then continued. "This is not good, you know. If he really is some childhood friend of Lord Danbridge then we are really going to need Sylvia's camera to expose this guy."

"Yep, it's not like we can waltz into Spyrius headquarters and expect them to take the word of two unknown college kids over some lifelong friend."

We stood there looking at each other for a moment. I broke the silence.

"Okay, it's eight thirty on a Sunday morning. We're in the middle of a stranger's house in suburban California. If we're going back in, we need to figure out how long we should wait."

"Couple of hours?"

"Who knows?" I said. "They could be camped out waiting for us to come back, or we could have spooked them and they are all back through the Town Square portal by now. That's where I assume they came in."

"I say we give it two hours. Any longer and who knows if this Kyle and Sarah could get back here some other way. We'll just have to be careful. Meanwhile, according to that Google thing, there's a grocery store a few blocks from here that opened at eight o'clock. I say we get a bite to eat."

I agreed and we carefully left through the back kitchen door. The last thing we needed was a neighbor calling the police. It was about a mile walk down the classic Route 66, the main road that runs along the northern edge of the Claremont Colleges. It was a beautiful warm, sunny day and we fell into the friendly banter and ribbing that was normal for the two of us. I think we both wanted a break from trying to figure out what to do with our situation. After all, we had two hours to kill.

We had almost arrived at the grocery store when Sylvia called me. I was going to call her soon anyway, once we got away from the busy road. I updated her on what we decided to do. She was worried about us but understood. We made an agreement that if she had not heard from us by Monday morning at the latest she would do everything in her power to get in touch with Lord Danbridge, even if she had to threaten to expose the *Oz* program. After all someone, possibly the Phil person, was supposed to come to the apartment Monday morning and force us to switch places. Though we could not assume Phil actually knew about *Oz*, someone at Virginia Tech working with Spyrius did. Larry was sulking, and they had agreed to head back to Tech soon. After some back and forth with Kyle, we recommended that they leave the projector in the back of Sylvia's car. This would keep it in their possession yet close enough to where they could get it and give it to these people if need be. What Larry would say was the wild card and Sylvia was hoping he would be in class when they came. Either way, Kyle and I couldn't worry about that at the moment. We promised to keep in touch.

We bought some breakfast sandwiches since it was still morning in California. I also bought a fairly large butcher's knife that the store had for sale. Kyle didn't really like the idea, and for that matter neither did I, but after what happened I figured it would be prudent to have at least some kind of weapon for protection. Not that either of us knew how to fight with a knife if push came to shove. I added it to our backpack. With time to waste we took a long way back, walking through campus, which was fairly scenic for the middle of suburbia. Neither of us had ever been in California before, so we were having a little fun playing tourist. I thought it was odd that for all the times Kyle went to Las Vegas for DefCon with his dad, they never made a side trip to California.

"My dad? Please, he's not like your dad who would just say, 'let's go and play family tourist somewhere.' If it's not related to his work, forget it. Of course he's been out to Silicon Valley a bunch of times but, except for DefCon, I'm not invited along."

"Sorry."

"Not your fault. That's why I want to come along for your annual beach trips. You know that."

Indeed I did. Every year our family rents a place at a beach for a week in the summer. Outer Banks, Virginia Beach, Myrtle Beach, and Disneyland once. Kyle has come along ever since the summer between our freshman and sophomore years at high school. I like it because it's more fun than just having my little sister to hang around with, and my sister likes it because she now gets to bring one of her friends along after she put up a fuss the first year Kyle came. The point is, as much as Kyle sometimes annoys my mom and dad, they realize that Kyle does not have much of the warm, loving family dynamic, and so they bring him along.

We went back to the house and carefully snuck back in. By then it was almost 10:00 and we figured there was no point in waiting around any longer. Either it was safe to go back in now, or it would never be.

"We came out at Yorke House," I said. "But the camera is somewhere between Town Square and Greenwich, so I say we go in at Greenwich, if we can, and trace back from there."

"Why not start at Town Square? That's probably inside the church and I kind of want to see what that looks like from the inside."

"Yeah, but it's also the central location. If there's going to be people around, that's where they would probably be. Plus that's where the bad guys came from. I think Greenwich would be much safer."

"I know, I was just hoping you wouldn't think about that," Kyle said sounding a little dejected.

"But you did, so that means… Oh, never mind. Let's go."

The laptop was still running so all we had to do was plug the projector back in, fire up the *Oz* program like usual and pick Greenwich. The portal came up and thankfully no bad people came out. We waited a moment just to be sure and then I stuck my head through to see where we were. I knew we weren't in Yorke House because the colors were slightly different, so I assumed it was Greenwich.

"Hopefully it's right around here so we can just run in, get the camera and then run back out here. Then we can figure out our next move. So no sightseeing this time, okay Kyle?"

"I may be less cautious than you, but a big guy with a gun chasing us is not my idea of a fun time. Don't worry."

And with that the two of us entered Oz.

We stood there for a bit after we came through; everything seemed quiet. Not a sound to be heard. Then we both noticed that the storeroom in the back was much brighter than the other times we were here. Last time that room had a dull light coming from a single fixture in the ceiling, but now it was bathed in a bright white light.

"That's odd," Kyle said as he started walking toward the room. "If it was like that when Sylvia came here maybe they went in and put the camera down without realizing it?"

"Wait a second, Kyle. Let's think about this. They were in a big hurry. Why would they take a side trip? And by the way, did you ever notice that while there are lights in these rooms there are no light switches anywhere?"

"Yes, I did notice that. Think Josh. By the time they got back here they probably realized they were not being followed, so they had some time."

"Okay, let's take a quick look, but remember, curiosity killed the cat."

"And satisfaction brought him back."

Like moths to a flame we entered the storeroom. Everything looked the same as before, except the light was much brighter. We went only a few steps before everything went black and our situation turned very, very bad.

Chapter 10

It was black. Pitch black. Not like someone turned just off the lights but like there was a total and complete absence of light. I could not see anything, not even Kyle, who had been only a foot away from me a second ago.

"Kyle, you there?"

"Yes, right here," he said as he hit me with his hand trying to find me. I grabbed his hand if for nothing else as reassurance that he was actually there. I couldn't see the end of my own hand.

"Alright, stop a second. Don't move. Okay, keep holding my hand, I'm going to turn us around and walk back through the door to the main room. It's only three feet away."

I proceeded to do that, but after only two steps I hit a wall. A wall I knew was not there a moment ago.

"What the heck? Kyle, grab ahold of my shirt with your other hand. I'm going to get the flashlight out of the backpack."

"Okay," he said with some obvious fear in his voice.

Kyle took hold of my shirt with his other hand as I let go of him, swung the backpack off, took out the flashlight and swung the backpack back over my shoulder. Meanwhile Kyle took his phone out with his other hand and turned on a flashlight app. With both lights on we looked around. We could finally see each other but there was nothing else. This place was no longer the storeroom we were in, this place was completely black. The walls were so black we could not make out where they were or how large the room we were in was.

I had no idea what was going on or what to do, but neither did Kyle, so I took the lead and did the best I could.

"Let's walk with my left hand on the wall here. Hold on to my right arm with your left hand, you can use your phone light with your right."

Kyle nodded and I slowly started walking, carefully and deliberately placing each foot on the ground just to make sure the floor was there, as I could not actually see it. I had Kyle hold on to me because it provided the only basis to reality. It felt like we were floating in outer space because there was no reference our minds could latch on to. The wall were black so we could not visually see what we were in.

Counting steps and turns around corners, it did not take too long to map out the room we were in. It was about twelve by twelve feet square. The ceiling, if there was one, was at least eight feet high, as I could not feel it jumping up. There were no doors, windows, ventilation shafts or anything. With nothing better to do, we combed over every square inch of the place just hoping upon hope that we would find something, anything that might help us out of this situation. But there was nothing. I tried chipping at the wall with the knife, but nothing. It was hard as rock. Eventually we just sat down next to each other. We had to turn off the flashlight and phone light to save batteries.

We sat there for at least a half hour trying to make sense of the situation. The general theory we came up with was that since this seemed to be some sort of artificially generated world, there would be nothing to stop the creators from generating a blank room like this one. We surmised that someone generated this room and then led us into it, probably that Cho guy because he seemed to be the technical one of the bad guys. They obviously had a reason for getting us out of the way. What we couldn't come up with was any ideas for getting out.

With nothing else to talk about, we just sat there in the dark, alone with our own thoughts. This in itself could be a dangerous thing. About two years ago I started having a pain in my side so I went to the doctor, who found a cyst on my side near my liver. I went in for surgery, and it was major surgery, which in itself was pretty scary, but everything worked out fine. I now have a little scar on my abdomen. What was most terrifying was during the first day of recovery when I was on morphine I started having the weirdest and scariest thoughts and dreams. It felt like I had lost control of my mental processes and was going crazy. I got over it pretty fast and stopped using the morphine; the physical pain was far less frightening, but it made me understand what insanity would be like. At the time I really didn't get it, but after taking psychology last year I got deeper understanding of what the mind was capable of.

After sitting in this dark room for another half hour, alone with my thoughts and contemplating the unthinkable prospect of my own mortality at only eighteen-years-old, some really weird things started creeping into the corners of my mind. I started thinking about how long we could hold out. We had a few snacks, but more importantly we only had a sixteen ounce bottle of water for the two of us. Even if rationed that would only last one day. That's assuming we were getting fresh air, without which we wouldn't last more than a day or two. I thought about odd things like what I would do when I had to pee. I hoped one corner of the floor was slightly slanted down so it would stay there. I didn't relish my last few days sitting in my own (and Kyle's) urine. I even started to think how glad I was that I bought that knife. I really scared myself on that one, but in reality if it ever got to the point where it got that bad I would rather be able to end it on my own terms. The other thing I was not sure of was how long my sanity would hold out. After the experience in the hospital, I knew that if this went on long enough my grasp on reality might go before my physical body did.

At that point I was so wrapped up in thinking about myself that I didn't notice the sobbing coming from Kyle. If I was worried *I* was going to lose it, then Kyle, who was a little emotionally fragile to begin with, was really in danger. I realized he was who I needed to be worrying about.

"I really messed up this time," Kyle dejectedly said.

"What do you mean?"

"I mean this is all my fault, Josh. I was so busy thinking about my own excitement that I didn't care one bit about what might happen to me or to you. Damn, Larry was right all along. But would I listen? No. I'm smarter than ninety-nine percent of the people on this planet but yet I'm so messed up. Why?"

By this time Kyle was sobbing hysterically. "Kyle, it's not your fault. I went in to this…"

"No, Josh," he interrupted me, "I'm messed up. You know that. You and Sylvia sit and talk about all how screwed up I am, how my parents don't love me, how immature I am, how needy and clingy I am."

Oops. I didn't think he knew about that.

"Yes, Josh. I've heard you two. One night when I was over and you thought I was sound asleep I heard you go on forever about my neuroses. I'm not upset though. You're right: I'm messed up. Heck, I've even heard you tell people at parties that I'm autistic, even though you know I am not, just because then people accept why I'm a pain and annoying. Oh, he's autistic, so I'll let him slide, even though really I'm not. I'm really just an annoying pain."

Oops. I didn't think he knew about that either.

"My bad, Kyle, there's no excuse for that."

"No, that's okay, I understand. Now I'm probably going to die, and I've never even been laid. Hell, I've never even kissed a girl."

Kyle was starting to lose it. "Stop, Kyle!" I yelled as I reached over and put my arm around him. He was trembling. "First, we are not going to die. We will get out of this situation."

That was something I was not so sure of myself, but I needed to say something.

"Second, I've never gotten laid either. So we are in the same boat on that one."

Kyle sniffed a little and took a deep breath, calming down a little. "But at least you had a girlfriend."

That part was true. Near the end of my junior year I started going out with this girl named Sally. She was in some of my classes and we were friendly and had some things in common, both a bit nerdy, but it was never more than that. Then one day one of her friends convinced both of us that we were made for each other and would be a perfect couple. So we started dating. It was fun. We got along, went to dinner, movies, a concert; even fooled around a bit. Overall we had some good times, but as summer came along we started seeing each other less and less. We didn't live all that close to each other, and then at some point we just stopped getting in touch with each other. When I saw her the next year we waved and smiled but never really talked to each other. I don't think either of us wanted to deal with explaining it. But it was nice to have actually had a real girlfriend, at least for a while. It made me a little more confident that there were people out there for me and I didn't need to stress over it too much. I think she kind of felt the same.

During my time with Sally, Kyle was a pain in the ass. He was simply jealous that suddenly my time was being shared with someone else. I got pretty mad at him, yet I also understood his point of view. I'm hoping that as he gets older and more mature it will be smoother next time. That is, being in this situation, if there ever was to be a next time.

"We're going to get out of this, Kyle, and don't be hard on yourself. I'm just as much to blame. I also wanted to do all of this. And don't think I don't feel guilty too. Don't get mad, but I've always thought of you as kind of a little brother. I mean I am not the most worldly, charismatic person in the world but I've always tried to kind of help you be more sociable and just have a more fun life in general. I didn't do my part too well this time either."

Kyle just gave me a hug. But I knew we couldn't just sit there. We had to keep busy.

"There's got to be a way," I said. "Let's go over this place again. Maybe we missed something."

We went over the place inch by inch again, but found nothing. Neither of us could think of any way out of this. We sat back down but this time I forced us to stay mentally active. We played stupid little games like twenty questions, told jokes and made up some stories. We would start reminiscing at times, but I tried to steer away from that as it would only make us more depressed and aware of our situation. Eventually we ran out of things to do. Kyle just kind of slumped over, leaning against me. I put my arm around him. By then it had been several hours, probably three, maybe four, since we had gotten into this situation and by that point I really did have to pee. But I didn't feel like moving. I didn't feel like doing anything.

"If I'm going to die, I'm really thankful you are here," Kyle said. "There is no way I could face this without you."

I didn't really have the energy to say anything. I just gave him a squeeze. Though I thought it was funny the way he worded it, as if he would rather me be there to die as well. But I knew what he meant.

And so we sat there.

And waited.

And then the light came.

Chapter 11

I'm not sure how long it had been, I think I might have actually dozed off for a bit, but suddenly there was a bright light and an angel silhouetted in it. I wasn't sure if I was dreaming, or maybe I had already died, but I remember thinking that the light was very bright and annoying.

"Kyle, Kyle Frost, are you okay?"

That didn't sound like an angel to me. It sounded like a girl. A very real and alive girl. It didn't look like an angel either, at least not the traditional depiction all in white with wings and floating above the ground. Once my eyes started getting used to the light it started looking like an ordinary girl dressed in ordinary clothes. In fact she looked about our age, like someone I would go to school with.

"Kyle!" she yelled when neither of us responded.

I could feel Kyle shaking his head as if to clear the cobwebs out and make sure this was real.

"Yes, what, huh? Yes, I'm Kyle. Who are you?"

"You don't remember me, do you?" the girl said as she walked toward us, almost as if she were a little annoyed that Kyle didn't instantly recognize her.

By this time she was standing right over us. She was definitely about our age, fairly pretty and dressed in casual pants and a black long sleeve shirt with the Spyrius logo on it and a Spyrius badge clipped onto it. She had dirty blond hair that hung just below her ears and small stud earrings, but not much else in the way of makeup or accessories. A bit of a tomboy look to her.

"No, I'm sorry. Am I supposed to?" Kyle said as we both started to get to our feet.

"I guess not," she said. "It's been a couple of years but I was in the DefCon kid's camp with you. I saw you there last year but I didn't have the guts to come up and say hi."

Kyle paused as if he was reaching back into the recesses of his mind, "Yes, I remember you. Darlene, right? I always thought that was an interesting, cool, name."

Darlene Hoffman was the name written on the Spyrius badge. I wasn't sure if Kyle truly remembered her name or just noticed it on the badge.

"Why would anyone not have the guts to say hi to me?"

"You? Come on, you're Andrew Frost's kid. You were with your dad. Like I was just going to walk up to you. Always thought you were cute though."

"What?" That came from both of us. By now we were both standing up and fully awake but totally confused as to what was going on.

"Darlene," I said. "Not that we aren't incredibly grateful that you are standing here right now - we are, believe us - but what exactly is going on?"

"Ah, yes," she replied. "There is a lot going on that you don't understand, but frankly there's a lot going on that we don't understand that you hopefully can help us with. Like, why you are here in this, whatever this is? But first, I am Darlene Hoffman, you are?"

"Joshua Amandil, call me Josh. Nice to meet you, believe me."

I shook her hand, and Kyle did the same. I think he was blushing a bit.

"Right now we need to get out of here. It took Dan and me almost two hours to find you and make a passageway to here. Come on, we've got about a twenty minute walk. I can fill you in on things along the way."

We left through a hole that now had appeared in the side of the room. It led into an endlessly long hallway that was just as featureless as the room we were in, except that it was white and gave off a soothing light. Kyle actually complained that he had to use the bathroom, something I seconded, but we both said we could hold it after Darlene asked if we could.

"You know, you caused quite a stir when you went out the Yorke House door that Kyle and Sarah came in through. We expected that to work fine, but you are the first humans to test that out. Kyle and Sarah were none too happy when they realized they were stranded though! I think that's kind of funny in a mean sort of way. Not that you would have known any better, then again you probably should have never been allowed to be in Oz in the first place. I was on the fence, not that my opinion would have mattered, but it was only because I recognized you, Kyle, that we didn't shut your access down after you surprised everyone and when you entered Oz in the first place. How did you figure that out, anyway? And more importantly, how did you get into that room?"

I think Darlene said that in one breath. She definitely talked fast. A bit of the nervous type. Both Kyle and I looked at each other not sure of all she was talking about and not knowing what to respond to first.

"Timeout," I said, making the timeout hand signal. "One thing at a time. Where are we going right now?"

"Umm, well I guess I can tell you because you're going to see it. You're going to the church basement, actually a sub-basement. There's a semi-secret emergency back door there. Not everyone on the project even knows it's there, only the people that actually have the rights to enter Oz: Dan, the head programmer and Sebastian of course. Oh, and now me, as of this morning, and now you two. That's how Kyle and Sarah got out, which triggered the alarm that brought all of us into work this morning."

"Darlene, we have something really important that we…"

"Kyle!" I said, abruptly cutting him off. "Excuse me one second, Darlene. I need to speak to my friend."

We stopped and I walked Kyle a few steps away out of earshot. "Do you think we can trust her?" I asked Kyle.

"Do we have a choice?" he answered. "I mean, did she not just rescue us? I'm pretty sure we can trust her. But don't panic, I wasn't going to tell her anything, just that we need to find something. I would much rather have that video camera first before we start making accusations. I think we can trust *her*, but that doesn't mean she will believe *us*."

"Okay, good. Though she does seem to like you."

That made Kyle blush again.

"Sorry about that," I said to Darlene. "Let's continue on, and can I ask the question the two of us want to know the answer to most?"

"My phone number?"

Kyle and I were not quite sure how to respond.

"I was making a joke. Obviously not a very good one. Okay, what question?"

"What is this place?"

"You mean this passageway, or Oz in general?"

"Oz in general. What *is* it?" I pressed.

"Well isn't it obvious? Kyle, come on, you're really smart, right? It's a virtual world running as a computer program that you can physically enter and be a part of. Actually, I was just giving you a hard time. I wouldn't expect you to know that. What is it? Well, it's probably the greatest leap forward in technology since, well, I don't know. I sometimes forget how mind-blowing all this would seem to any but the two dozen or so people that have been working on it. After all, I have been working on it constantly for the past year. But you're computer hackers, at least you are, Kyle - sorry, didn't mean to assume anything, Josh - so you must have at least had an idea."

"Well obviously it was an artificial world of some sort," Kyle pointed out, a little defensive. "But what we don't know is how it works. What's running the program? How do the projectors work? How does a complex carbon-based life-form go through that portal and still stay in one piece?"

"Portal?"

"The big purple door the projectors make," I said.

"Oh, we just call them doors. I like 'portal' though. I think it's a better name, and it would alleviate the occasional confusion when talking about real doors versus the, well, portal doors."

She smiled and then continued. "Okay, you want the grand overview of how Oz works? Be prepared to keep up, I can talk really fast. Ready?"

We both nodded in the affirmative.

"Okay, here goes. About four years ago two molecular biologists in Sweden made an incredible breakthrough. They created a machine that scanned, for lack of a better word, inorganic or organic matter, compiled all the billions of atoms, examined how they interact with each other and then recreated that within a virtual computer world. The organic matter, or live beings, could roam free in this world. They started with earthworms, but trouble is you can't get an earthworm to come back out, so they trained rats to go in and then come back out. When the rats came out their essence was reconstituted, incorporating any changes that happened while in the virtual world. But they ran into two problems. One, rats cannot talk and therefore couldn't report after they came back out and two, to do this on any greater scale they needed a lot of money."

"Enter Lord Danbridge," Kyle said interrupting Darlene.

"Yes Kyle, but no one really calls him Lord Danbridge, that's just for the press and public. He got that nickname in college, but he just likes being called Sebastian. I don't think he wants people to think he's somehow better than them or above them just because he's rich so we are all on a first name basis. I mean everyone, even the janitors. He just does the Lord Danbridge thing for the press just for kicks. He plays up the slightly mad Howard Hughes image for fun, too."

"Back to Oz," I nudged her slightly.

"Oh, sorry. So the two scientists, Oscar and Sven, teamed up with Sebastian, who had come into his oodles of money fairly recently and was looking for something important to do with it. Now they realized that this technology not only had important implications, but that it could be used for nefarious purposes and could be very controversial. So it was kept a secret. To do that Sebastian formed Spyrius, a computer company, which has been pretty successful as a computer company, but in reality is just a cover for the Oz project."

She paused for a second allowing us to soak things in.

"They built a bigger world, Oz 1.0, and they used cats. They would do brain scans before and after, temperament tests and such, and everything seemed fine. The next step was humans, but to do that they needed more power. By power I mean raw electrical power. You have no idea how much power Oz takes to run. So they located Spyrius at Moses

Lake, Washington, which has an abundance of cheap and dependable hydroelectric power and is fairly remote and therefore less accessible to prying eyes. Chuck Harper was the first human to go through. Funny story, he always went by Charles, but after he entered Oz he told everyone to call him Chuck in honor of Chuck Yeager, the first person to break the sound barrier. This was Oz 2.0 and he came through fine. Following me so far?"

We both replied in the affirmative.

"Oz 2.0 had really nothing inside of it. Just a blank space, kind of like the corridor we are walking down now. A proof of concept. So the next step was to create an actual world. So they, well, we because by that point I was part of it - my father was the original architect and I was kind of adopted as a mascot, but also I am a pretty mean programmer… Where was I? Oh yeah, we created Oz 3.0 which is a 3.2 mile circular city, so to speak. It's divided into twelve sections like a pie, each named after a place in London. Naming them after London was just a lark or so I am told by the way. Anyway, you have those twelve sections plus the middle Town Square, which isn't square at all. Each section plus the square has an entry/exit point. Obviously the projectors create the door, I mean portal, which allows you to move into Oz. I think that covers the high points. Any questions?"

"Seriously?" Kyle responded. "About a million. How does the projector work?"

"How it works in the biological sense I have no idea. But it takes the input scanned, and that's a terrible term but I can't think of anything better, and sends it to the main computers that then allow you to enter Oz, either by direct connection for those at the office, or now over the Internet using a proprietary protocol and unique compression algorithms. A copy is transferred to the portal in the church basement as a sort of backdoor, literally and figuratively. A little computer joke there."

"We got it," I said.

"Oh and by the way, the program checks for sufficient bandwidth, but when you moved the projector to wherever you moved it and put it through a proxy in the Cayman Islands you really were pushing the limit of it. We never thought to put in a check for a proxy!"

"Yeah, that was my idea," said Kyle. "We were worried someone was going to find us and take it away."

"I wonder if that was why it seemed a little harder to go through at Sylvia's than at Tech or when we came out in California."

"Quite possibly," Darlene said. "Oh, and yes, we did send someone to get you last night. We were running some tests yesterday morning using the Wembley portal, and no one was supposed to be inside, when all of a sudden you, Josh, just pop in to Oz. Freaked us all out. We had to stop the tests immediately. We were going to shut you down but then you came through, Kyle and I recognized you. At that point Sebastian was more curious as to what you were going to do than alarmed that you were there. But we still needed to get to you, if nothing else you had a video camera on you and we couldn't let that get out. By the way, where is that? We are going to want that video, you understand."

We ignored that request for the moment, not wanting to tell her that it was probably sitting in Oz at that very moment.

"So you can see us when we are in there?" I asked.

"Sort of. Remember Oz is a program, so we can monitor everyone and track where they are at all times. Though only at the portals do we have actual video where we can watch what people are doing."

"Stop, we'll be exposed," I whispered to Kyle. He shook his head as he got it, remembering what that Cho person said when that Bradley guy ran after us. They were using something to block the ability for them to be tracked while in Oz. We kept that to ourselves for the time being. Darlene continued on, seemingly forgetting about her camera question.

"So we asked Evan, the guy at Tech who was supposed to have your apartment, to go to the apartment to get to you. But he was staying at a friend's an hour away and by the time he got there you were gone."

"I thought his name was Phil?"

"Phil? Who? Oh, I get it. No, he's just some lackey that we sent to get you to switch rooms. Didn't work obviously. He knows nothing about Oz. Evan Duncan, he's a new guy. He's an agriculture guy. Seems Virginia Tech is a big agriculture school."

"Yes it is," both Kyle and I stated.

"He's going to work on actually growing plants and such in Oz. You may have noticed that there is nothing alive in Oz as far as vegetation right now."

"Wait a second - the room was in the name of Eliza someone or else that's something to do with some old program," I said.

"Yeah, I never heard of that either. Some name Sebastian came up with, some old computer program. Just keeping with secrecy so the room could not be traced back to Evan."

"Kyle got it," I said, giving a little plug to my friend, who just smiled.

"Cool. Anyway, I told Sebastian who you were, Kyle, and who your father is. He recognized your father. Read one of his books or saw him speak once. So I guess Sebastian got curious and he wanted to actually see what you all did in Oz. So we kept it open for you. Not sure if that was wise or not, but you are alive. Anyway, that afternoon you reappeared, with two other people at that, but then you seemed to retire for the night. So who are those two other people anyway?"

"Sylvia and Larry," I answered. "They are my roommates, and boyfriend/girlfriend. At least they were. Not too sure right at this moment…"

"Ah, okay. So continuing, we figured you would go back in this morning, and a few of us were going to come in to see what you were up to, but before any of us got in we got all the alarms for Kyle and Sarah having to use the emergency back doors. What you did was risky. We'd never had a human go out a door that someone else came in through. We assumed it would work, and we tested it with cats, but we had yet to try with a human. Guess it works!"

"What are you talking about?" I said.

"When you go in it copies all of your genetic material and such, and everyone always went out the same door they came in. But now we have multiple doors - sorry, meant to start using portals - so you could go out a different portal than the one you came in through. We are all made of the same stuff per say, so theoretically you should be able to go out a different portal and the program could reconstitute you as yourself, but we had never tested it. Until now," she said with a quirky smile.

"And since we shut the portal down Kyle and Sarah could not get back out," Kyle said.

"No. I mean yes, that too. But even if you didn't shut it down they could not come out. It's a one for one thing. One person in, one person out. If two go in, only two can come out of that portal. In fact, before shutting down the program checks to make sure an equal number came out that went in. That can be overridden. That's another reason for the safety backdoor: just in case something happens."

"Now hold on," I said. "What if something bad happened when we went through that portal in California? What if we didn't come out as ourselves? For that matter, how do we know we are okay right now?"

"Well, you got me there. We never thought you would come out a different door! But you seem okay, right? I'm sure we can give you a full battery of medical tests when we get back if you want. But my turn now for a question as I think we're almost at the church. Just why did you go out a different door? And just as important, you went back in at about ten this morning and then immediately disappeared off the face of the, well the face of Oz, and Dan had to find you in that room that's actually outside of Oz proper. What happened there?"

I put up my hand to Kyle telling him not to say anything. I wanted to be careful about what we said. I still did not want to tell the whole story until we got our hands on that camera.

"About that. Tell me real quick, when we get to this room under the church what are we doing?"

"We're going through the backdoor portal to our offices in Moses Lake. There are a few people who want to talk to you."

"I'll bet," Kyle said to me, but just loud enough for Darlene to hear.

"What?" she said looking at Kyle.

"Never mind. Look, when we get there can we get up to the church and back out to the outside area?"

"Well, yes, of course. The door to the sub-basement is only hidden from the upstairs."

"And we can then come back down to that basement?"

"Well yes, you have to put both your hands in a particular place. I've never done it but I was told what it was this morning before I came in to get you. But I'm not supposed to go up, I'm supposed to bring you straight back to Spyrius."

I looked at Kyle to pick it up from there. Darlene didn't know me from Adam, but she seems to have some level of trust in Kyle. One of the good things that comes from constantly hanging around the same friend for five years is that they can usually pick up on where you are going.

"Darlene," Kyle said. "When we get to the church, we need to do something first."

"What are you talking about?"

"You asked what happened. Something did happen, but we need to check on something before we tell you the whole story. You've got to trust me."

At this point I could see something not far ahead of us. I think we had finally reached the church basement. Darlene stopped and thought for a moment. I got the distinct feeling that she was not telling us everything she knew, or maybe more precisely what she suspected might have happened.

"Fine. I'll trust you, but I'm coming along."

Kyle and I looked at each other. I could really see no reason why it would matter if she was with us. It was an extremely remote possibility that she was in cahoots with that ringleader, Randy Hanson, guy, and if she was it would be pretty hopeless anyway. I shrugged at Kyle, he shrugged back.

"Okay," I said. "Tag along."

I think she knew that she was not going to get any more information from us until after we did whatever it was she might have thought we were going to do, as she didn't ask us any more questions.

The church basement, or sub-basement, looked like a dank, dark medieval dungeon completely made of stone. On a table, also made of stone, there were several Spyrius laptops, tablets, a couple of phones and assorted accessories. In the middle of the room was a portal, though this portal was about twice the size of a normal portal. There were a couple of rooms off to the side and stairs leading up to a big, wooden door.

"So are these computers and tablets brought in, or are they created in this world?" Kyle asked.

"Yes, created in this world, so they are not technically real."

"So these are really virtual machines!" Kyle said laughingly.

"Darlene," I hesitantly spoke, "not to bother you too much, but I really, really, need to use a restroom."

"I second that!" exclaimed Kyle.

"Oh, no problem. Right through that arch, though they are just pit toilets. Keeping in line with the time period. There is toilet paper if you need it, just drop it down the hole."

Pit toilet or not, after use Kyle and I felt much better. But that did beg the question that I posed to Darlene, "So our, you know, organic waste matter, where does it go?"

"Good question actually. Before about two weeks ago there were no working bathrooms - you weren't allowed to go! Right now everything goes into a virtual holding tank kind of in its own space. There's a plan to see if it can be recycled and used within Oz itself, and I think that is something that Evan Duncan guy is going to work on. You know, using manure to grow the plants. Not something I have any desire to get involved in! So are you ready to do whatever it is you need to do?"

"Ready," we both said.

"Better be good because I know I am going to get in trouble for this."

We walked up the stairs and out the door, which opened into a proper church basement. From the basement we could see a pair of curved stone steps leading up to the main floor. Odd thing was that the door from this side was just stone like the wall. We closed it about half way, as Darlene wanted to test the way to open it.

"Remember, I have never done this," Darlene stated. "Let me make sure we can get back in. Okay, you go to the end of the wall, count up four rows of stones, two over and put your left hand on that stone. Forty-two, yes, they're a bunch a geeks that programmed this. Then go two rows over and four up. Easy to remember, at least. Bit of a reach though. Okay right hand here."

There was a slight hum and the door opened fully. "Good," Darlene noted as we closed the door fully. When closed, the door blended into the stone. It was invisible.

We went up the stairs to the main floor and I remembered that ringleader, Randy Hanson, stating that the inside of the church still has a lot of work to be done. He was right. There was an altar and two rows of pews, but not much else. The windows did have the stained glass but all the decorations and extras that you would normally see were missing. I couldn't tell you exactly what, as I had never been inside a European church, but it just felt empty.

"The church shell is one of the original buildings, but it's a slow process in building it out," Darlene noted as if she read my mind.

One addition was a portal, right by the altar. This one was normal sized and it was pretty obvious that this was the Town Square portal. We were not there for sightseeing though and so we walked down the rows of pews and out the front door.

We stood in the Town Square, which looked the same as it had this morning. No one was there, thankfully. We walked around until we were facing the Greenwich area and Kyle, with his near photographic memory took over.

"They were in a hurry and a bit panicked, so I am going to assume they went back exactly the way they came, down the Royal Mews road and not the Hyde Park road we used yesterday."

"Worst case: we get to the portal and don't find it, so we circle back down the other road," I said.

We started down the spoke road between Greenwich and Royal Mews. We walked at a good pace, but not running as we were constantly scanning to see if we could locate the camera. Darlene, who was plenty talkative on our earlier trek kept quiet, as did Kyle and I. I had a million more questions, and I am sure Kyle did too, but right now all that mattered was finding that video camera. For whatever Darlene was thinking we were doing, she kept it to herself.

After about fifteen minutes we came upon Sylvia's chalk marks turning into the Greenwich area proper. Darlene did remark on how good an idea that was. She took her phone out of her pocket and showed us an app that had a real-time map of Oz so people would not get lost. Something she noted that we would not have had. We turned into Greenwich and on the second turn from the spoke road we saw Sylva's video camera, still attached to the headband, lying on the ground in plain sight.

Chapter 12

"Well I'll be," Kyle stated.

"Wow, I wasn't expecting it to be that easy."

"I bet you I know what happened," continued Kyle. "This is only the second turn from the spoke road. They were running full speed and as they took the turn it slipped right off her head. It's not like that headband is that secure. And with the endorphins running through them at that point they never even noticed."

I picked up the camera and checked to make sure the memory card was still inside, which it was. One part of me could not believe we were that lucky, but on the other hand it made sense that the camera would still be lying here.

"That's going to show us what happened this morning." Darlene stated as if she assumed it to be fact.

"Because," Kyle was surmising, "you don't know what happened yesterday. Part of what we did this morning is missing from your records."

She nodded, looking a little puzzled that Kyle figured that out.

"Is there someplace we can go where we are not being monitored from outside?" I asked Darlene.

"The church sub-basement. We have to go there anyway." she answered.

I put the camera in my backpack. "Let's go."

We walked as fast as we could without actually jogging, as we all wanted to get back to the basement. The mood was a little lighter because Kyle and I were relieved that we had the camera. We would be more relieved when we were sure it had recorded the earlier incident at Town Hall.

"So, tell us about the buildings." I inquired. "Why all the identical storefronts? What's up with the twelve brick buildings, and what about the church?"

"The storefronts, as you call them, are just placeholders. The idea is to create twelve totally unique areas eventually. Oz 3.0 is only a few months old, and it was much easier just to take a couple of variations on one building, copy and paste it all over one area, and then copy and paste that section eleven more times. As I mentioned, my father is the architect for all that you see so far, though we now have a second architect to help out. We even wrote a custom CAD program called Oz Creator to help in design and creation. It actually interfaces with the Oz code itself so you can make changes and have them appear in Oz. That's what I have been working on since I got here. It's basically my dad's and my program; he's a pretty good programmer, too."

"We tried running it," Kyle noted, "but it said we didn't meet the requirements."

"Oh yeah, we have some pretty hefty workstations with huge monitors that we use for that. I'll show you how it works when we get back."

We found out a little more about Darlene as we went back. Like Kyle she too was an only child and a bit of a prodigy. She lived with her dad, who became a single father when her mom died of cancer a few years earlier. She graduated high school at sixteen and it was that confluence of events that led her and her father to basically start a new life in Moses Lake. It seems her dad was friends with an old co-worker who was in with Sebastian, or something like that, leading to an offer to be one of the original Spyrius employees working on the Oz program. Darlene's father had the skills both as a programmer and an architect so he was a perfect fit. At first Darlene was taking classes at the Community College in Moses Lake, but that didn't challenge her at all. She contemplated leaving for a real university but she was also secretly helping her father with the original programming of the Oz Creator program. Once Sebastian realized how much work she had done, and how good she actually was, he offered her a job, even though she was only sixteen at the time. So school was put on hold.

"And that's what I've been working on for about a year now. I love the work. The only thing that sucks is that I'm the only person my age. I mean everyone, or most everyone, is great, but it's kind of hard to identify with everyone else. Most of them are in their late twenties and thirties, with a few, like my dad, even older."

"Why not leave and go to school somewhere? Then you'll make tons of friends." Kyle offered.

"I have a couple friends. I have one friend I met at the community college. She's a couple years older than me, and we go to movies, parties, etcetera. But life here is so different than what I am used to. I grew up in L.A. This is a small town mentality and it is very different. But the point is, what we are doing here is groundbreaking. I feel like I'm one of the original seven astronauts; it's that game changing. How can you leave something this monumental? I just wish there was someone else around my age working on this."

She said the last part very obviously looking at Kyle. I definitely think he was feeling a bit uncomfortable with the attention from Darlene. I thought that was pretty funny.

"How old are you then?" I asked

"Seventeen. Turn eighteen in a little over a month."

We arrived back in the Town Square are and headed into the church and down into the sub-basement area. We saw no one during our excursion. Everything seemed to be going smoothly.

"Shoot," I said as I took out the camera. "The battery is dead. Makes sense as it just kept recording after it fell off Sylvia's head."

"It uses a regular memory card, right?" Darlene asked.

"Uh, yeah."

"Plug it into this computer."

And so I did, making a copy onto that computer first. Everything seemed to be there with all the video intact. I got the video cued up to the point where we were just about to notice the group. Meanwhile Kyle brought up the picture of that group that he took with his phone.

"Darlene, do you recognize the people in this picture? And what can you tell us about them?" he said showing the picture to Darlene.

She looked at the picture with puzzlement. "Not the best picture, but that's Randy Hanson, he's one of Sebastian's closest friends and head of security. The guy with the laptop is Cho Park, a programmer. The big guy: I don't know his name but I think he's one of the guards. But who are the other two in the suits? That's the church in the background. Is this in Oz? None of them have the rights to be in Oz by themselves, though Randy certainly has the access to do it. What's going on here?"

"I think you need to watch this video," I said.

And with that I played the video. You couldn't really see anything, mostly Sylvia had the camera pointed toward Kyle and I behind the cart, but you could hear just fine. Pretty much everything Kyle and I heard from behind the cart Darlene was hearing. After we were discovered Sylvia did manage to move the camera around the wall she was behind just enough to see the group yelling and chasing after us, including

Bradley waving the gun. As soon as they turned the corner down the spoke road after us and went out of sight we watched Sylvia put the camera on her head and then run off with Larry back to the Greenwich portal. Larry was in full sprint saying some not very nice things and Sylvia was having a hard time keeping up. We fast forwarded a bit until they turned in and then the camera flew off onto the ground. There was nothing else after that until the battery ran out.

"Well?" I said to Darlene, who was obviously in a state of disbelief.

"I, I don't know what to say. This seems so implausible, and I'd say you were somehow making this up, but it explains what happened this morning. Why the four of you literally disappeared for a while right during that time period."

"So you had no idea that they were in Oz this morning?" Kyle asked.

"No, there was nothing."

"So is it possible that Cho guy had some sort of transmitter that basically made them invisible to your monitoring while inside of its range?" he continued.

"I really don't know. We need to speak to Dan about this. He can figure it out and then we need to show Sebastian."

"Dan, the head programmer guy?" I asked. "How do we know we can trust him?"

"Dan? He's the only reason you're not still stuck in that odd place," Darlene said in a defensive tone. "You know how long it took him to track you down? Someone was hiding that room real well. And probably the same person that... We need Dan."

"Okay, sorry," I said. "Nothing personal. Heck, we weren't even sure if we could trust you at first! It's just that Lord Danbridge's, sorry,

Sebastian's best buddy is trying to sell this technology to terrorists or something and then someone tries to, well, eliminate us, we're not sure who to trust."

"Got it. No, Dan is like a big brother to me, and he's been trying to figure out what happened. Plus he's no fan of Randy, in fact neither am I really."

"Why?" asked Kyle.

"Randy's known Sebastian since they were kids. But from what I guess they kind of drifted apart for a while. When Sebastian started Spyrius he handpicked Randy to head security. He's a bit of a jerk, but I think Sebastian likes him precisely because he will make the hard decisions and be ruthless if needed. This way Sebastian doesn't need to."

"Kind of like the rich nerd hiring the class bully to be his bodyguard."

"Yes, Kyle, something like that. I don't know the whole story as I wasn't here from the beginning and don't interact with Randy much at all. Dan could probably tell you more; he was here from the beginning. Either way we need to get this to Sebastian soon so he can see it and Dan's the best bet to help explain what they did. After I went in to find you he kept working on figuring out who made the room and how. Hopefully he has figured out something by now."

"What exactly was that room?" Kyle asked.

"To be honest, I don't know. We all watched you as you went back in this morning, but you were only there for a few seconds. You walked into the other room and then you just vanished. We, and by that I mean Dan, Sebastian and I, had just traced what you did that morning and how the four of you walked from Greenwich to the Town Square and then you just disappeared for a while. Then after a bit you reappeared running to the Yorke House portal, while your two friends reappeared running toward Greenwich."

"When you say watch us, what do you mean by that?" Kyle asked.

"Well we are not really seeing you, except at the portals where there is a video feed, like I said, but we can track anyone's movement at any time, either through a map on the computer screen or this really cool three-dimensional holographic model of Oz that I will show you. Since we know the genetic makeup of all our people that go in we know who is who. Obviously we made up tags for you all, except Kyle, of course, since I knew who you were."

"So back to that room," Kyle prompted Darlene.

"Yeah, so at first we just assumed there was some weird glitch in the tracking program and that you would reappear, but after something like a half hour, and knowing you didn't come out somewhere, we went to find you."

"How did you find us?" I asked.

"Well it was all Dan, like I said. The actual Oz code is huge and we program with a specialized language Dan made that creates the actual code. It's just too big to code manually. So Dan had to go into the actual base code and do comparisons with code from a snapshot taken before. He eventually found an extra small room of sorts that somehow was manually created and which resided just outside of Oz proper. Kind of like a room pasted on to the outside of Oz, but with no connection. And we saw that you two were inside of it."

"But we walked into that room within the backroom of the Greenwich storeroom. So how did we get outside of Oz?" asked Kyle.

"Yes, we also wondered how you disappeared from one place and ended up somewhere else. Then Dan did a few tricks and found a subroutine that deleted itself. What it did was it created that room within the room in Greenwich, then when someone triggered the subroutine the room was actually moved to outside of Oz and the actual subroutine that did it deleted itself. Fortunately, Dan created the program such that anytime code changed a copy was created to Dan's personal space. This was more to troubleshoot any accidental coding errors by the programmers, but came in handy here."

"So how were you able to get to us to get us out?" Kyle prompted.

"Dan created a totally new passageway that ran under Oz to connect the church sub-basement to that room. He didn't want to just open it for you since we didn't know what you would do, so he was going to go in and get you himself."

"But you got us," I stated.

"Yeah, I used my charm," she said with a devious smile. "I do not have the rights to go into Oz myself. I had only been in a couple of time with others and I didn't know about the sub-basement part at all. But I used my charms to convince them that since Kyle knew me I would be the best person to go get you two. It took a bit of convincing, but they were putty in my hands! I'm just thankful my dad wasn't there."

"Why?" asked Kyle.

"He's a bit scared of Oz and doesn't go in himself. Didn't really want me to go in at all, even just for a couple guided tours, but he finally relented on that. But he's in L.A., ironically to help Sarah with architectural stuff as she, unlike my dad, will actually go into Oz. You probably just missed him. I am sure he was just waiting in his hotel room and was going to go over to their place when they were done in Oz this morning. Anyway, so Dan took me to the hidden portal at Spyrius that leads to the sub-basement under the church and I went to find you. I wasn't really supposed to go out of the sub-basement, but he showed me the trick to get back just in case. He probably was pretty mad when he saw us come up, but I think he will understand when he learns what's going on. Anyway, we need to get out of here and back to Spyrius."

"Sounds good," I said.

"Follow me then,"

We followed Darlene though the super-sized portal in the middle of the room and came out in a small room. Taking a quick look around revealed a fairly small room that didn't have much except an extra-large portal that we just came through, and, behind it, a projector that was twice the size of the other two projectors we had seen. It had a hard-wired electrical cable providing the power. Next to it was a rack of servers, one of which was connected to the projector. Some network cables ran along the ceiling and out of the room. There were no windows and the room was a bit noisy from the air conditioning necessary, I assumed, to keep the equipment cool. The room looked like a modern server room and there was a set of stairs leading up to a door.

"This is the super-secret room," Darlene said. "I didn't even know about it until today."

"Why is it so secret?" Kyle asked.

"I'm not totally sure, but Dan was saying that he and Sebastian set this up as the emergency exit, as I said earlier. Those who come into Oz via other portals can come out through here in an emergency, but only Dan and Sebastian and maybe one or two others can actually enter this room from inside Spyrius headquarters. Dan keeps some backups of the Oz program on the servers in here too. He said that except for testing at the beginning, today is the first time this portal has been used, and now it's been used twice in one day!"

We exited the room, followed a non-descript hallway, went up a set of stairs, down a short hall and then into what was obviously the main control room for the Oz project.

"Now this was what I was expecting," I said.

This room was a large, clean, state of the art room filled with computers and large monitors on the wall. It looked like one of those computer control rooms in TV and movies. Dominating the middle of the room was the circular, three-dimensional holographic model of Oz that Darlene had talked about earlier. Beyond a glass wall was another large room that was obviously the main server room as it had rows and rows of racks with servers in them. There were no windows to the outside, not that I expected any. Only three people were in the room, even though it could fit many more. One young lady was busy doing work on one of the workstations; she barely looked up when we came in. The second was a guy who looked like security, and he did get up when we came in. The third was a guy, probably around thirty, with short, cropped red hair and an average build. He kind of looked like a slightly older, redheaded version of Larry. All three people were wearing Spyrius Technology badges clipped to lanyards hanging around their necks.

"Darlene, where have you been?" the redhead said with a slight hint of anger, mixed with concern. "You were supposed to come straight back up with these two once you found them."

The security guy who was coming toward us stopped once it was obvious that the redhead, who I assumed was Dan, was expecting us. The guard probably was concerned since Kyle and I were not supposed to be there.

"Good to see you too Dan," Darlene said. "Dan, meet Kyle Frost and Joshua, uh, I forgot your last name."

"Amandil"

"Amandil, Joshua Amandil. Kyle and Josh meet Dan O'Brien. Yes, he's Irish, by the way."

"So you are the famous Kyle Frost," Dan said without any hint of an Irish accent. "I have heard so much about you from Darlene in the last twenty-four hours."

"Dan!" Darlene exclaimed, obviously not happy at that remark, as Dan shook Kyle's hand. Kyle didn't quite seem to know what to make of that remark.

"And hello to you, too, Josh," Dan said in a very friendly manner as he extended his hand to me, shaking with a strong and firm handshake that made me seem a bit inferior.

"Now, Darlene, you need to tell me what's been going on from your end," he said in a suddenly serious demeanor.

"Where is Sebastian? Is he in his office?" Darlene asked.

"No, he's disappeared with Randy and Cho."

Chapter 13

Kyle and I looked at each other with that 'this does not bode well' look. Darlene looked like she was about to leap out of her own skin.

"What do you mean he disappeared with Randy and Cho!"

Dan looked a little taken aback at Darlene's sudden excitement. "Calm down, though yes, something is very strange. Randy and Cho came in saying that they had to show something very important to him. I didn't think much of it other than wondering why they were here on a Sunday, but about ten minutes after they left here they went into Oz through the Whitehall area. Then the odd thing, they went across to Smithfield and then exited Oz out of the door in Smithfield."

"How could you let them do that? Wait, what do you mean exited out the door in Smithfield? You can't do that!"

"One thing at a time. First, why would I be concerned about Randy and Sebastian going off, they do that all the time. I had nothing to be concerned about, except that now that they went in and out of Oz I do. Second, somebody or somebodies have been messing with the code in ways they should not have been able to without permission, kind of like what happened with that room these two were stuck in."

"What do you mean?"

"Someone started the projector at WSU and a copy of those three was transferred to it much like," he lowered his voice, "the emergency door. And they went out that door at WSU."

"Could we follow them if we needed to?" Darlene asked.

"No, that's the thing. The projector is not online now."

"Okay, this is really not good," Darlene said. "We need to go to your office now."

She said that with such authority that Dan looked taken aback. But he realized she probably had a good reason and so with a quick 'follow me' from Dan we went with him down the hall. Kyle and I were a little lost. I had no idea what 'WSU' was, but I figured we would pick up on these things soon enough.

Dan's office was good sized and full of random laptops, servers on the floor, papers, shelves of programming books, charts and maps of Oz on the wall, and other things you would expect in a head programmer's office. There was a secondary room off to the side, though I could not see what was in there. There were no outside windows here either, and after Dan closed the door he pulled down the shade to the window on the door.

"Memory card Josh," Darlene commanded to me, to which I obliged. "Put this in one of your machines," she said looking at Dan, "there is a video you need to watch real quick. Oh and look at this picture," she said as Kyle, with some forethought, handed her his phone with the picture of Randy, Cho and Bradley the security guy.

Dan went through the same routine with us that Darlene had earlier, watching the video with us filling him in on some of the finer points. This time we stopped right after Sylvia and Larry got up to run back as there was no need to go any further. Dan sat there for a second as he obviously processed what he just said and tried to figure out what the next move was.

"I told you, I never liked that guy," he said empathically.

"Because he's a bully?" Kyle asked.

"I filled them in a little," Darlene added.

"I don't know if bully is the word. But from the beginning, and remember Randy and I were the first two hired on, Randy seemed to have a different view of this from the rest of us. Everyone else here, including Sebastian, really thinks of this as an altruistic project, something to expand the horizons of mankind and hopefully have tangible benefits. I mean Sebastian does pay us well, but we are working long hours in a small town in the middle of nowhere. Maybe someday we will be able to profit from this, but no one here is doing this just for the money. We all see a bigger purpose. Not sure what, but something that will hopefully change society for the better. But Randy just doesn't seem to see it that way. To him this is just a job, one where he has a lot of power. To be honest I am not surprised at what I just saw, I almost expected it."

"Power corrupts, absolute power corrupts absolutely."

"Exactly Kyle. Very good saying by the way."

"Lord Action," I said.

"Huh?"

"Lord Action, that's who the quote is from. Some British Lord from the nineteenth century I think."

"Oh, still good. Anyway I am not surprised he would try to profit from this in some way or another. What I wasn't expecting was how grandiose his plans are, how he has obviously recruited others, and that he's willing to kill for it! That's not good at all. We need to find Sebastian, but unfortunately it looks like they are in Pullman."

"Pullman?" both Kyle and I asked.

"Pullman, Washington," Darlene interjected. "It's where Washington State University, or WSU, is. We have a person working on the Oz project there."

"How many universities are working on this?" I asked.

"Just Harvey Mudd, remember Sebastian and some of us went there," Dan noted, "WSU, as it is fairly close to here, and now Virginia Tech - our first foray across the country. We only got this working remotely over the Internet a couple months ago."

"So Dan, what to do?" Darlene asked, obviously expecting Dan to have perfect insight.

"I think we need to get to Pullman and fast. I already checked the video of them going through the door to WSU and it doesn't look like Sebastian suspected anything at that point. I don't think they are going to do anything to him immediately, but I just don't know. I really don't know what they are doing in Pullman."

"Why don't we just call the police, or FBI or someone?" I asked.

"Not sure what that would do, even if they could find them. Maybe they were meeting someone there. After all obviously someone turned on the projector. I think it's a little too early to get the authorities involved, and they would start asking some uncomfortable questions. We'll keep that as an option though if push comes to shove. I really wonder about Cho, he's a good programmer, but is he good enough to do all the sneaky things that have been going on? I'm not sure."

"Did you figure out who made that room that Kyle and Josh were put in?" Darlene asked.

"No, I've been too busy figuring out how they went through that door in WSU. I just found the code someone made to copy people, lifted straight from the code that makes a copy for the backdoor in the church basement we put in. Someone's really been going over the code and I don't know who. We have eight other programmers besides Cho and I, and I just can't imagine it's only Cho."

"You just told me this morning that you needed an extra powerful portal to make the copies and that's why that secret portal in the church basement is so big," Darlene stated.

"Portal?"

"Oh, yeah, that's what Kyle and Josh call the doors. I like it better at it allows us to differentiate from real doors. And it sounds a little cooler too."

"Okay, fair enough. Yes, if you're making copies and keeping tabs on dozens of people going through dozens of doors at once, which may happen someday, but right now a regular door will work. The backdoor in the church was made bigger from the beginning since it stores a copy of everyone who goes through any of the thirteen other doors - portals - whatever."

"So how do we get to Pullman?" Kyle asked. "Go through another door?"

"No we can't. Someone would have to turn the projector on at that end, and obviously I don't trust the guy over there right now. We will have to do it the old fashioned way. We will drive. It's a little over two hours. Darlene, take these two back to the main room and wait for me. I need to do something first."

Darlene didn't ask what, so we didn't either. Dan gave me back the memory card, he had made a copy onto his laptop for himself. On the way back to the main room Darlene showed us one of two rooms that hosted projectors for opening portals to Oz. Back in the main room Darlene went over and made some small talk with the other programmer, a light skinned African American with long hair probably in her late twenties. Kyle and I just sat quietly together with the security guy staring at us the whole time but doing nothing. Dan came in shortly with a backpack and motioned us out. We followed him down the hallway, Darlene stopping to get a light pullover and her backpack. The backpacks had the Spyrius tablet/laptop combos that they took everywhere with them.

"One thing I did was to set it so the WSU projector cannot connect to Oz so they will not be able to enter from WSU. There is no way they can override it, though if we need to I will be able to."

I was pretty sure he did something else, but whatever it was he was not telling us.

"Let's get to my car and get out of here. It's past four now, so we won't get there until six thirty. We'll run through a drive-thru to get some food, I am sure you two are hungry after being in the room for four hours, but that's the best we can do right now."

Four hours I thought, was it that long? I guess I did doze off. I was pretty hungry though. "No complaints," I said with Kyle responding likewise.

We went up an elevator and exited to what was obviously the main rotunda for Spyrius Technology proper. It was very impressive, though empty on this Sunday afternoon. Any other time I would have loved to take in the grandeur, but not today. Dan gave a little wave to the building guards, who looked a bit puzzled at the presence of Kyle and myself, but never had a chance to ask anything. As we were leaving I did say one thing to Dan I didn't want to forget.

"Dan, I just want to say, uh, thanks for saving us back there. It was getting pretty bad."

"Don't worry about it. We can discuss it all over a beer later, but right now, well actually you're not old enough, right, either way we have to concentrate on what we are going to do right now."

"I second what Josh said," Kyle said a little meekly, probably just wanting to forget the time in that room that already felt far longer ago then just an hour.

It was fairly warm out, a little surprising considering how far north we were, but good considering Kyle and I both had only long sleeve T-shirts on. It will probably get a little cool when the sun goes down I thought.

"Call Sylvia," Kyle reminded me.

"Good point, almost forgot, she's probably worrying. Yep, she called a few times."

I explained Sylvia and Larry to Dan real quick and then placed a call to Sylvia. They were back at Tech, after all it was after 7:00 back east, and she seemed relieved to hear us. She said Larry had calmed down a bit but they really hadn't talked about the situation yet. I even heard Larry in the background telling Sylvia to say that he was glad we were safe. I didn't go into any detail of the situation we were currently in, just to say that we had some people on our side helping us and that everything should work out okay. I told her that obviously Kyle and I would probably not make the start of class the next day, but there was not much we could do. I handed the phone to Kyle at her request and after a few pleasantries Kyle hung up and gave me the phone.

Moses Lake is a small town of about 20,000 people. The closest real city anyone knows is Spokane about an hour and a half north east. Pullman sits about two hours slightly to the south.

Spyrius sits slightly north of the actual town of Moses Lake, near the lake itself, which looks more like a river at that point than a lake. The drive down Route 17 actually bypasses the town proper so Kyle and I missed that, though we did pass the airport only a few miles from Spyrius itself where Dan pointed out that Sebastian kept a private jet, complete with pilot.

"Normally I take Route 17 to 26, the first half is flat and straight through farmland and then some twists and turns to Colfax. More interesting a drive. But we're in a rush, so I'm heading up on Interstate 90 to Route 23 to Colfax then down Route 195 to Pullman. We can really fly on the Interstate."

We did stop by a sub shop right by the entrance to the Interstate and got some much needed food to eat in the car and headed off onto I-90. Just like this morning when Kyle and I took our little walk, there was nothing we could do about our situation in that moment, so we figured we might as well keep it light and enjoy each other's company. I had a question about one thing that I had been noticing as I went through that various different portals.

"Question Dan. When I went through the portal at Tech I felt a little resistance, but not too much. When we were at Sylvia's in Roanoke, going through the proxy, there was definitely more resistance, but the one in the church had none. Does that have to do with the throughput?"

"You nailed it exactly. A lot of data is compiled as you walk through and the faster the connection the faster and easier you can go through. Roanoke, that's somewhere in southwest Virginia, right? Is that where you took the projector? Is that where it is now?"

"Roanoke is about an hour away from Tech. It's where Sylvia's folks live. About that projector, it got a little broken. The lens got shattered, it was an accident."

Dan just sighed. I guess he figured that now was not the time to worry about that.

We got to know Dan a little better on the drive and I could see why Darlene liked him so much and looked up to him like a big brother. Dan just seemed to be one of those genuinely nice guys, and very charismatic. The kind of person you just liked being around. Turns out

Dan actually is Irish, like actually born in Ireland. But he moved when he was an infant, hence the American accent. His parents moved to Atlantic City, a common place for Irish immigrants, before eventually moving out to Los Angeles. He went to Harvey Mudd the same time as Sebastian and though they weren't really friends they knew of each other. Sebastian was a couple grades ahead and an Engineering major but Dan was like a whiz kid programmer so their paths occasionally crossed at competitions and such. Enough so that when Sebastian was spinning up Spyrius he called Dan to see if he was interested, and Dan was. One of the very first hires and the original programmer for the Oz project.

"He remembered that I coded a custom complier once at school, creating my own language," Dan recalled. "He knew the first thing he needed for Oz was someone to create the language that we would use to program it. So that's how I got here."

Seems Dan was engaged before coming out here and had to pick between his fiancé and working for Spyrius. He didn't dwell on that much and I was not going to pry, but it did make me realize both Dan and Darlene's dedication to what they felt was a pivotal technology breakthrough for humanity, and what they both were giving up personally for it.

We filled Dan, and Darlene for that matter, in on how Kyle and I met and knew each other and gave them the background on Sylvia and Larry. Spending the time with Dan also allowed him to become more comfortable with Kyle and me. I mean we were just some random 18 year old college kids who out of the blue he had to not only rescue but suddenly take the word of. Of course having a video and Darlene vouching for Kyle at least helped, but the trip I think got him comfortable enough to accept us as part of the team, at least temporarily.

"You know at some point we will need to talk to your two friends Larry and Sylvia about what they went through and what they saw,"

Dan said. "There is a real reason for secrecy on this, and we need to help them understand that they need to not go talking to everyone about this. But that's for later, we have more immediate concerns now."

"I have a question," Kyle said. "What about the laptop that Cho guy had? Is that what was somehow blocking your ability to monitor them?"

"Seems so," answered Dan. "What I think it does is basically cancel out the markers that make up the person and transmit out a blank field for any person that stands within its range. That why your team disappeared too while you were in the range. I'll be very interested to get ahold of that laptop."

Eventually we got off the Interstate and moved to the twisty, windy two lane road that makes up Route 23. Being late on a Sunday afternoon there was little traffic and soon the car became quiet and Kyle and I both nodded off to sleep in the back seat. It had been a long and eventful day and who knew how much more it had to offer.

Darlene woke us up just as we were coming down a big hill that led into Pullman proper.

"You two both slept for almost an hour back there."

"I was awake for most of it," Kyle said. "Just relaxing, and I didn't want to wake Josh, he needs his beauty sleep you know."

I elbowed Kyle in the ribs. He yelped but smiled, and we ended up elbowing each other back and forth until Dan told us to stop acting like little kids. It was a bit of normalcy in a very unusual day, which was nice as I knew we would have to get back to the reality of the situation real soon.

It was 6:30 at this point and the sun was low on the horizon looking like it was going to set within the hour. I would have loved to have just called it a night right there, but I knew we couldn't do that.

"So where exactly are we going?" I asked.

"We're going to the house that has the portal first and see if anyone is home and take it from there," Dan said. "It's across from campus proper on the other side of town."

"Who from Spyrius works here, and what do they do?" Kyle asked.

"Only one, his name is Eusebio Regalado. He's from Spain and teaches here at WSU. He implemented the ability to use the doors, sorry, portals over the Internet. He has a projector here so he can test various protocols, compression algorithms and the like. He doesn't go into Oz himself, but he has test equipment he pushes in and out to measure how fast the coding and decoding goes back to the main computers. He lives alone with his dog. He uses his dog for the testing, I've been out here a couple of times to help him."

"His dog?"

"You have to have something organic to go through to do a real test."

We had to drive through downtown Pullman to get to the area where the school and this guy's house were at. Pullman, along with its next door neighbor Moscow across the border in Idaho, are not quite city size, but a bit larger than a town. Washington State University is a major NCAA division I school with an enrollment of over 25,000, not much less than the population of Pullman proper. It reminded me a lot of Blacksburg, where Virginia Tech resides. Both are college towns, isolated from other big population centers and about the same size. As we skirted the campus, it too reminded me of Tech. We could see the last remnants of students unloading cars and settling in for the new semester.

We winded our way through a subdivision and passed the house. Dan pointed it out. It looked like something from the 1970s with that very angular and pseudo futuristic looking architecture that looks very dated now. It was set back from the road a bit, with a lot of trees around so it was almost hidden. From what we could see it looked dark inside with no cars in the driveway. It didn't look like anyone was home. Dan drove down the street a little and parked his car among some others across from some community garden that looked like a part of WSU.

"Dan, what are we actually going to do?" Darlene asked.

"That's a good question. I know you think I have all the answers, but I don't. And I am worried that it could get dangerous. I brought a Taser just in case, but we need to be careful. Let's walk up there and see if we can see anything."

We walked back up the block with Dan leading. We were all quiet and I was getting a bit nervous. I was just a wimpy college student, I was not a trained spy used to dangerous situations. When we got to the house it still looked empty.

"Wait here, I'm going to walk around the house," Dan said.

We waited on the sidewalk trying to look casual as to not attract the attention of any neighbors. None seemed to care. Dan whistled and signaled us to come down, which we did.

"No one is home. I'd love to get inside but the doors are locked and I don't want to break a window or something."

Kyle and I both chuckled. "That will not be a problem," Kyle said confidently. "I can open these doors in thirty seconds. Time me."

Dan looked puzzled, Kyle said to trust him, and we went to the side door, which was the most secluded. Kyle took out the lock picking kit and I would say it took him about twenty seconds to get through the standard door lock that was probably twenty years old at least.

"Well I'll be," was all Dan could say.

I handed Dan the flashlight I had so we didn't have to turn on the lights. We had entered through the kitchen and were quickly attacked by a very friendly and excited golden retriever. Dan told us his name was Franco, which I found a bit odd as I thought the Spanish didn't like Franco, and Dan scratched him a bit and calmed him down. We quickly made our way through the living room and down a hall to a back bedroom where the projector was with Franco in toe. We could turn on the light there since no other house was in view. There was a cage (for Franco we assumed) on wheels with a rope and a laptop with sensors attached to the top. Dan pointed out that this is what he used for testing.

"What are you looking for?" Darlene asked.

"I'm not sure," he answered. "Anything that might lead me to where Sebastian is. Let me see…"

The projector was off, but Dan logged into the computer that was connected to it. He had an overarching password that worked on all the computers for the Oz project.

"Nothing much here. The logs show that they came through earlier and then they shut the projector off. But we already knew that."

"Now what?" I asked.

"Eusebio has an office on campus. Maybe they are there. I can't think of any other place to try. Only trouble is that I don't want to call him first and the doors into the buildings are locked on a Sunday night. Kyle, how good are those lock picking skills of yours?"

Kyle just smiled. He was loving this.

"Okay then, let's go."

We drove into the heart of campus only a few minutes away, parking in a lot right near the new football stadium. It was Sunday evening so there were not too many people about. We walked to a nice academic building caddy corner to the stadium and went to a side door. Kyle worked his magic right there in the open, but no one was about to notice. This time it took a couple of minutes before he got the door open.

"It was a little trickier," Kyle said.

The door opened into the stairwell and we went up to the third floor. Dan wasn't too sure where Eusebio's office was, he had only been to it once, but after a few wrong turns we finally found it.

Looking through the windows in the door Eusebio seemed to be alone. There was no sign of Sebastian, Randy or Cho. Dan shrugged not knowing what else to do, knocked on the door, opened it and walked in.

"Dan, what are you doing here?" Eusebio said with a heavy Spanish accent. "Did you come through with everyone else?"

He said this very naturally and went to shake Dan's hand in a friendly manner. It didn't seem like he was trying to hide anything.

"Uh, no," Dan said. "So did Randy and Sebastian come through the door earlier?"

"Sebastian came? I guess, though I don't really know for sure. Randy called me this morning asking me to turn on the projector here. He said they were testing a whole new process allowing someone to enter at one place and exit at another."

"Did you see them come thorough?"

"No Dan. I have work to do here, see all those," he said pointing to a bunch of electronic components mounted on a wallboard. "I'm testing throughput on different routers, so I've been here all day. I went home, booted the laptop, turned on the projector, and opened the door to

Smithfield like Randy asked. Then I came back here. By the way how did you get in? I thought the building was locked on Sundays."

"Someone was coming out so we went in the open door," Dan said thinking quickly on his feet.

"Well, I'll be here another hour, but if you're staying you and your friends are welcome to grab a late bite with me. Who are your friends? I don't think we have been introduced."

"Oh, sorry. Where are my manners? This is Darlene, who works with us."

"Ah, Darlene, I have heard about you, so nice to finally meet you."

"And these are Josh and Kyle who are helping us out."

"Nice to meet you too."

"We will probably have to take a rain check on dinner. Do you have any idea where they might have gone to if they were not at your house?"

"I assume you went by my house? If they were not there then they might have gone back into Oz. Otherwise I don't know, though I know Sebastian loves that homemade ice cream place around the corner, but I think they are closed today. Did you come through the door or drive?"

"We drove. We, uh, thought something was wrong. They must have gone back through Oz. We'll head back to Moses Lake. Sorry to bother you, we'll get dinner next time."

"No problem at all. See you later."

And with that we left. We waited until we got outside until any of us spoke. I broke the silence, "So Dan, do you believe him?"

"I'm not sure what to believe, but it certainly could have happened the way he said."

"He almost sounded too friendly and his answers too pat. Or maybe I've just seen to many detective TV shows. You know him though."

"Well not too well at all actually. I've worked with him out here twice. I think he only came to Moses Point once."

"Did he know about the emergency portal, the one where the copies are made?" Kyle asked.

"No he didn't, because he never actually went into Oz so we decided he didn't need to know. Why?"

"He said they were testing a new process allowing someone to enter at one place and exit at another. If he knew about the sub-basement portal he would have already known that was possible. So I guess his response makes sense."

"He doesn't deal with that anyway. He's only about what protocols, ciphers, compression algorithms etcetera are most efficient for moving data. But one thing we know for sure is they didn't go back into Oz, because I fixed it so they wouldn't."

"Back to the house?" Darlene asked.

"I guess, we'll wait there until they come back. If they are not back in a while then maybe we will call the authorities."

We drove back to the house following the same procedure as before, driving past and then parking down the street. Walking up to the house it looked just like it had earlier, empty. We had re-locked the side door and Kyle made quick work of unlocking it again. Inside Franco left up on us just as before. We went into the spare bedroom, Dan sat in the lone chair by the desk while Darlene, Kyle and I sat down on the floor. Dan checked on his laptop just to make sure nothing weird happened, but no one had entered Oz. We kept the light off and were just going to wait, for a while at least, we had no other plan.

"So what's with the dryer plugs for the projectors?" Kyle asked just to kill some time.

"These projectors take a lot of power," he answered as he got up to check the laptop connected to the projector. "They need 240 volts and 30 amps to run, so we put dryer plugs in. For this house and the one at Harvey Mudd we have batteries for backup in case there is a power outage. For the apartment at Tech Sebastian worked out something with the builder to put the plug in on a separate circuit with a separate backup in the basement. Not sure how - hey! Wait a second. Someone turned the projector on while we were out."

"I think I hear something!" Darlene exclaimed.

Dan whirled back around and went for his backpack, grabbing something. The three of us stood up from our sitting position. Someone else was definitely in the house.

Chapter 14

"Move it," we heard. It was definitely Randy's voice and a second later Sebastian, whom I easily recognized from pictures, entered the room with Randy right behind. He had a fairly large gun pointed at his Lordship.

"Over there by your friends," Randy ordered Sebastian, and he walked over to where the four of us were.

The spare bedroom was fairly small and Dan was sitting in the chair by the desk at the far wall of the room as you walked in with his laptop in his lap. I think he took out the Taser and had it under the laptop, but I was not sure. Sebastian was standing next to the desk and myself, Kyle and Darlene were next to Sebastian in that order. Against the side wall was the projector on a stand pointed to the empty middle of the room. Franco's cage was off to one side. Randy had moved inside the doorway and was facing all of us from about 10 feet away with his gun.

"Well, what a surprise here. We have Mr. Goody Two Shoes Danny Boy, his little pet Darlene, and what a nice addition - two of the meddling little punks. How convenient that I noticed that the laptop had been moved when we were out getting some food, and when I called Eusebio he just happened to mention that you all just left his office. I had a feeling you would be coming back."

Randy was speaking in a very slow a deliberate voice, like someone who was a bit insane. To say I was scared would be an understatement, I was terrified. At least before in Oz we were occupied with running away from Randy, but here we were trapped. True it was five against one, but he had a really big gun and I had the feeling he would use it.

Just then Randy's phone vibrated. He picked it up and told someone to come on in. A moment later we heard the side door open and then Cho walked into the bedroom and stood beside Randy.

"Look who we have here Cho. It's a whole gang of busybodies," Randy then turned back to us. "After Eusebio called I had Cho move the car so you wouldn't notice. Perfect timing wouldn't you say?"

"Randy, let's put the gun down and talk about this," Sebastian said in a surprisingly calm voice.

"No!" shouted Randy. "You had your chance. I tried to reason with you over dinner, tried to make you see how we all could profit in the millions here, but you obviously want none of that. And don't tell me you've changed your mind, because I won't believe you for a second. Now Dan, what did you do so we can't get back into Oz?"

"I don't know what you are…" Dan started to say.

"Bull! We tried the projector, but it didn't work. Cho said it had to be your doing, but Cho's not quite smart enough to figure out what you did. I'll give you one more chance to answer me correctly or you will get a bullet in your brain."

"Dan, tell him whatever you did," Sebastian said to Dan. "He's not fooling around here."

Dan hesitated for a moment. "Okay, yes, I wasn't sure what happened when you took Sebastian and Cho and went in one door and out another here. So I locked it just to be on the safe side."

"Yeah, do you like how we figured out how to copy your structure when you go through and transfer it to another door? This allows you to move from one place to another, something my customers really want to be able to do."

"He wants to sell this technology to the highest bidder," Sebastian informed Dan.

"Really? These two said that earlier, but I didn't believe them," Dan said, probably trying to see if he could get Randy on his side, as he saw the video and definitely believed what Randy was up to.

"Sure you didn't. You've hated me from the day we met, and let it be known Danny Boy, the feeling is mutual. Now fix that thing so the projector will work and we can get into Oz."

"I can't do that from here, I have to go back to Moses Lake."

"He's lying," Cho said.

"Thanks Cho, but I think I can figure that out myself. Your laptop is right there. I know it's connected to the wireless, so get it fixed now or say hello to that bullet."

"Just do it Dan," Sebastian said.

"Sure?" Dan asked quietly back to Sebastian.

"Yes."

Dan opened his laptop and started typing. Kyle, Darlene and I were all staying very still and not saying a word throughout this, Sebastian and Randy just stared at each other and Cho just stood there.

"It's unlocked," Dan said after a bit.

"Okay, Cho, set up what we talked about."

Cho went to the laptop connected to the projector and fired it up quickly. A portal soon appeared in the middle of the room. He then went back to his own laptop and worked on it for a bit as everyone sat in silence before finally saying, "It's all working fine now."

"Good boy." He then turned back to us, "You know, we're going to make a fortune on this, but unfortunately that means that all of you will have to be eliminated."

He gave extra emphasis on the last word, and I think we all let out a little gasp.

"Cho, is the room all set like we talked about?" he continued.

"Yes," he said. "But…"

"Good," Randy said interrupting whatever Cho was going to say. "Now, all five of you, into the door, one after the other. Do it now or else."

"Or else what?" Sebastian asked.

"Or else I blow your brains out!"

"Look it's me that you have the issue with, not them," Sebastian said pointing to the rest of us. "Let them go and then do what you will with me."

"Good try Mr. Hero, but in order for me to see the fruition of my plans everyone has to die."

"Die!" Cho exclaimed, but this time Dan cut him off.

"I see five of us and one gun," Dan said starting to rise from his chair. "You won't get all five of us."

"Wait a second!" Cho yelled. "Randy, you never said anything about killing anybody. I never signed up for that."

"Sit back down Dan."

Dan and Randy looked at each other for a moment, indisputable hate in both of their eyes. Dan sat down, obviously figuring it was the best move for the moment.

"My little Cho. Just what did you think was going to happen? We were just going to sell this and everyone would be okay with it? This is the big time. And your hands are already dirty, those two twerps should be dying by now and you did that. Too bad they got rescued somehow. Not sure how that happened, but I am sure Dan did it."

"You said we were just going to scare them not kill them," Cho said, half stated like he was suddenly realizing that he was in way over his head.

"Please Cho, you're not that stupid. Or if you are then too bad."

Cho looked to Randy, then to the portal, then to us. He was obviously trying to figure out what to do. I am not sure what he was promised by Randy, but maybe, just maybe, he was realizing that once the technology was sold Randy wouldn't need him anymore. Either way he looked scared. His mind clicked into a base instinct and he ran for the portal only a couple of feet away from him. "Run immediately to the right," he yelled to us at he went to enter it almost diagonally from the left to the right.

I have never been next to a live gun being fired in my life. I knew they were loud, but I didn't know they were that loud. Randy fired his gun at Cho and right before he entered the portal a bullet impacted him in the back. The sound was deafening and I felt the shockwave in my own chest. The force of the bullet thrust Cho forward and he fell into the portal where he was swallowed up and disappeared.

With that moment of distraction Dan stood up flinging his laptop off and pulling out the Taser gun he indeed had in his lap, bringing it up, forward and then firing directly at Randy. Everything was a blur to me as I think my body was going into a state of shock. My legs were buckling under me as I stated falling to the ground, probably an unconscious response to get to the safest position possible. The prongs from the Taser found their target and embedded into Randy's chest. Randy's body convulsed and the gun flew forward from his hand landing only a foot from me, now down on my knees.

"Get the gun," Dan said and I instinctively reached for it and scooped it in towards me, sliding it behind me.

Randy fell to the ground, but like the police videos you see of people on drugs doing super human acts he actually pulled himself up a little, reached around with his right arm, screaming out like a banshee, and grabbed the prongs ripping them right out of his chest.

Dan and Sebastian both looked at Randy in shock, not sure if they actually saw him do that. True, Randy was a pretty big guy but still there must have been a lot of adrenaline for him to be able to counteract the convulsions. He sat there on his knees for a moment catching his breath and then looked at us. For a second it looked like a game of chicken, with each side waiting for the other to move. The gun, which I probably should have picked up, was behind me and out of immediate reach. Randy weighed his options for a second and then got up and ran into the portal with the same odd diagonal angle that Cho tried to enter. He was gone.

All five of us looked at each other for a moment in silence taking in what just happened. Darlene finally spoke, "are we just going to let him get away?"

"Don't worry," Dan said. "Two can play at their game. I don't think we want to follow right now, they have a trap set up in there and I need to find it and disarm it before we do anything."

"I assume that's what Cho was warning us about," I added. "I think he had a change of heart at the last minute and was trying to tell us to go immediately right to avoid the trap. Notice that's exactly what Randy did."

"What are you going to do about Randy?" Sebastian asked Dan. "I know you have something up your sleeve."

"You bet. He's got to go across to Whitehall to get back. When I rescued Josh and Kyle here I found the code for the room they created that held them. Before we left I set up another room and I can set it up where the Whitehall portal is and trap him. We have ten minutes at least."

"What room are you talking about, and what's a portal?"

"Oh, of course, you know nothing about what happened to Josh and Kyle here. Tell you later."

"Portal is what we call your doors," Kyle added.

"Okay, you get to that Dan," Sebastian said before turning to face Kyle. "And you must be Kyle Frost. I've heard a lot about you from Darlene in the last day, and certainly know who your father is, by reputation at least."

Now that things had calmed down Kyle was finally aware that he was in the presence of one of his tech heroes. Add to that blushing over Darlene's adulation he could barely look him in the face but managed to mutter a 'nice to meet you'.

Darlene headed off what would have been a slightly awkward moment by introducing me to Sebastian.

"Well good to meet you both and there's a lot I want to talk to you two about, but for now we have a bit of a situation. That was a very loud gun and I wonder if any neighbors called the police. And then there is Eusebio; Darlene, Dan, do you think he was in on this? I wasn't paying attention to who called who, I was busy working with Cho trying to figure out why the portal would not work."

They both replied that they were not totally sure but Kyle, with his excellent memory, spoke up.

"After Eusebio called I had Cho move the car so you wouldn't notice."

"What?" Sebastian asked.

"At first Randy said 'when I called Eusebio', but then later he said 'after Eusebio called'"

"And what are the odds that Randy called Eusebio exactly when we left?" I spoke continuing Kyle's thought. "It only took us five minutes to get here."

"Good catch. Well we still don't know the level of his involvement, but either way I want to take this projector with us. He was just tweaking things anyway, his main work is done."

"What exactly happened Sebastian?" Dan looked up from his laptop and asked.

Sebastian was about to speak, and then he looked at Kyle and I. "Kyle, Josh, forgive me for being blunt here. Dan, are we cool with these two?"

Dan stopped and thought for a second. Initially I thought I should be insulted, but Sebastian didn't know us from a hole in the wall so I can understand his reluctance to spill too much about what was going on without some conformation from someone he trusted to vouch for us. As for Dan he seemed to be the kind that sized a person up pretty quick and made a decision on their trustworthiness. I guess Kyle and I passed muster.

"Yes," Dan said very simply and matter of fact before going to his laptop. Obviously Sebastian had complete trust in Dan's opinion

"Okay then. Well it seems I've been played for a fool. And I thought I was such a good judge of character, I normally am, except for Randy. I guess that's what you get when you're too close to someone. He and Cho came in this afternoon at Spyrius, as you know, and wanted to show me something really incredible. So I agreed and then they took me in through Smithfield and we went across and out through Whitehall. Of course, well you know Dan."

"All three of them know about the emergency door in the sub-basement and how it works. That's how we rescued Josh and Kyle."

"Oh. Okay. You need to catch me up with what happened on your side. But anyway, that was nothing new to me, but I pretended to be impressed. I just wonder who did it."

"So do I. Because I don't think it was Cho."

"Anyway, we came out here and went over to this Spanish tapas restaurant in Moscow that Eusebio showed us once, then Randy did the hard sell on me. He was pushing me to accept selling this technology so we can make a lot of money even though he knows I am totally against that. I mean yeah, hopefully someday we can license some of this, but this is not just about making money. This is about furthering mankind. He ended the conversation with an 'it was worth a try' explanation, but I was starting to get the feeling he was up to something."

"Moscow?"

"Yes Darlene, that's the next town over, in Idaho. No idea how it got the name. So anyway, we came back here ready to go back across Oz, but that's when we found that the door here wouldn't let us though. That's when things started getting weird. Cho worked on it trying to figure it out. I tried to help, but I don't really know the programming code. Randy was getting really upset at Cho and after two hours we finally gave up and Randy took us to a bar for a drink and so he could think, or so he said. At this point I was getting real suspicious about what was going on. I couldn't see any reason why the door, umm, portal, I kind of like that name, wouldn't work unless you did something Dan. So anyway, we came back here and I went with Cho to see if the portal still wasn't working and that's when Randy talked to Eusebio. Then the proverbial poop hit the fan and he snapped. Suddenly he was a totally different person I had never seen before. He pulled the gun on me and told Cho to move the car. He then took me into the master bedroom and basically told me to be quiet or he would blow my head off. The odd thing though is I wasn't surprised for some reason. As if deep inside I never fully trusted him, even though he's been my friend since like fourth grade. So yes Dan, go ahead and say it."

"Say what?"

"You know. Say I told you so. You never trusted him and I thought it was because you were just jealous or something."

"Nope," Dan said laughing. "Not going to give you the pleasure! Okay now. Important stuff here. They had a trap set about a foot into the Smithfield room that would have put all of us into one of those rooms like Josh and Kyle were in. I removed that so we can go check on Cho now. I'm tracking Randy, he's going to Whitehall to get back to Oz. But he's going to have a nasty surprise when he gets to the Whitehall portal room as he will be sucked up into one of those empty rooms. That will hold him for now until we figure out what to do. Whoever wrote this code is good and I need to figure out who, but I'm a programmer, not a forensics specialist."

"I can help you with that," Kyle volunteered.

Both Dan and Sebastian looked at Kyle.

"Computer forensics is really just hacking in reverse. Instead of trying to break into something and cover all your tracks you reverse it to uncover the tracks and figure out what someone else did. And not to sound too arrogant, as that seems to be a problem with me, but I am pretty good. Probably better at that then actual programming. My dad taught me well."

"I'll vouch for him," I said.

"What, that he's arrogant, or a good hacker?" Sebastian asked.

Both of us stood there not sure what to say as we couldn't read if he was serious or not.

"I was just making a joke! Just trying to add a little levity to this very sober situation. Anyway, so it's safe for me to go in and check on Cho?"

"Yes, go for it."

Sebastian went in to check on Cho and came out a minute later. He just shook his head and said there was nothing to do. He was killed instantly and it was not pretty.

"We need to figure out what to do with Cho," he said. "He has no family in America and pretty much kept to himself. That's probably what made it easy for Randy to recruit him. I say we keep him there now and come back and get him out of Oz when we get back to Spyrius. I want to take this projector and laptop with me. I don't trust Eusebio. Anyone have an alternate plan of action?"

He looked at all of us, even Kyle and I. But none of us could think of a better plan of action.

"We need to wait until Randy hits Whitehall," Dan said monitoring him on his laptop. "Should be any minute now but I need to verify that he gets sucked up into that room."

"You will need to tell me about this weird room," Sebastian added.

"Does anyone else find it odd that no neighbor seems to have called the police after a very loud gunshot?" Darlene asked.

"Yes I did." Sebastian answered. "This house is somewhat secluded, but not that secluded. And I had this whole excuse that we were working on an electrical project for WSU and shorted something that caused a big bang."

"Apathy," I added. "No one want to get involved anymore."

"But you think there would be at least one noisy neighbor. There always is."

"True Darlene," Sebastian said. "But I am not arguing, it's one less thing we have to worry about. Hey Josh, you look the strongest next to Dan, help me get the projector down."

Calling me strong was a stretch, but I guess next to Kyle and Darlene I barely fit the bill. We started packing up the projector and the laptop that was connected to it when Dan suddenly chimed in.

"Got that bastard!"

"Just like Kyle and me?" I asked.

"Yes. He is trapped in a room of nothing, in the middle of nowhere. He's not going anywhere."

"Okay then," Sebastian said. "Let's get out of here before Eusebio gets back."

Chapter 15

Darlene went and got the car as Sebastian now had Dan to help with the heavy projector. Before they moved the projector Sebastian picked up the gun Randy used with some paper towels and carefully put it into a bag he found. He figured it would be best to take it with us. Since Cho was shot falling into the portal there was no blood in the room, and in fact there was no indication that any crime had taken place at all. Dan even found the shell casing and that was on the floor and put in the bag with the gun.

Kyle and I got Dan's stuff as well as Cho's laptop, which Dan said he was very interested in perusing through at some point. Both Sebastian and Dan took a moment to find Franco and say goodbye, probably thinking they would never again see the dog who had helped out in the experiments for Oz. He had gone into hiding when the gunshot rang out.

We all piled into Dan's car. Sebastian was in the front passenger seat leaving Kyle, Darlene and I to fit in the back. Kyle took the middle with Darlene and me on either side. The car wasn't that big so we were pressed against each other. I think Kyle was a little embarrassed about Darlene pressing against him but Darlene seemed to enjoy it.

On the trip back to Moses Lake we filled Sebastian in on everything that had happened on our end. We showed him the video from Sylvia's camera on Dan's laptop. He was pretty dumbfounded by that. We told him everything Kyle and I did with Sylvia and Larry and explained what had happened when we were trapped in the room and how Dan and Darlene rescued us. Soon he was caught up on everything.

"By the way Josh, where have the videos you took been copied to and you do have that video camera with you, right?" Sebastian asked me.

"Right here in my backpack," I answered holding up the backpack that I had kept with me this whole time, though I left it in the car while we were in Pullman. "It's only been copied to a virtual computer in that sub-basement and Dan's laptop you have now."

"Good. So, I hope you don't mind if I ask for the memory card? I hope you understand that I really don't want the videos you took floating around."

I understood, even though I really didn't want to give it up. For that matter I wasn't totally sure if Sylvia or Larry made a backup of the very first videos last night, but I figured I wouldn't mention that now. Sebastian noticed my hesitance.

"I will give you a brand new card as soon as we get back. Promise!"

"Well, it's technically not mine to give, its Sylvia's. But I guess under the circumstances she will understand."

I took the video card out and handed it to Sebastian.

As we continued, Sebastian filled us in a little more on Oz. At this point, like Dan, he seemed to warm-up to trusting Kyle and me, at least for the time being. After all we basically knew everything at this point anyway, and it was his fault in the first place for letting us roam around in Oz. He seemed to be a pretty down to Earth guy for a multi-millionaire, not that I had any previous experience with multi-millionaires. He was definitely not the reclusive Howard Hughes like person the press seemed to indicate. I guess Darlene was right that he just played that up for fun, or maybe it helped in getting him some privacy. Either way, to hard core tech geeks like Kyle and I Sebastian was a bit of a rock star, so it was really cool to suddenly be in his inner circle so to speak, even if it was by happenstance and probably only temporary.

"I have a question," Kyle asked of Sebastian.

"What?"

"Eliza Weizenbaum. Darlene said you didn't want to use that Evan guy's real name, but why did you use that name?"

"Oh, did you like that? I try to think of funny things like that. Did you get it? I liked that one, I've never been happy with Oz. Always thought it should have a slightly more cryptic name but never could think of a better one, and it's too late now."

"Yes, Eliza, the old computer psychologist program. I thought that was pretty cool."

"Yes, and we are doing some true artificial intelligence therapist programming at Spyrius anyway, so that name seemed appropriate. Good job Kyle, always fun when people figure out my sometimes arcane references."

Kyle had a wide smile on his face satisfied at the positive reinforcement from one of his heroes. The kind of simple positive reinforcement his dad never seemed to provide.

"So I have been wondering, why were you setting Evan up in our apartment building in the first place?" I asked. "Doesn't he have his own place?"

"Oh, yes, he had his own place, but unlike Eusebio at WSU and the Vaughn's in L.A. his place doesn't meet the electrical requirements. Fortunately they were building that new apartment building and while it's mostly meant for student housing I figured it would work fine for what Evan was going to do. So I used a few connections, greased a few palms and worked with the builder of that new building to add the extra outlet and backup system in the basement. Amazing what people will do when you offer them enough money!"

It was 10:30 pm when we got back to Spyrius headquarters. No one else was there at that time except the guards. We went down to Dan's office first and he checked to see if Randy was still trapped in the room.

"Randy is still there," he said. "By the way, what are we going to do about him?"

"I think we should all sleep on that," Sebastian answered. "Whatever we decide I don't think I am going to feel any guilt in letting him stew for the night in there. We'll figure that out and what we will do with Cho tomorrow."

"Feeling a bit betrayed?"

"Yes Dan. Quite a bit."

"Well then I'm going to poke around for a bit before I head home, but I really need to work tomorrow on figuring out who did this programming and how they covered their tracks. Kyle, you interested in giving me a hand tomorrow? A fresh set of eye may help, and to be honest I don't want to bring in any of the other programmers. Right now I am not sure who to trust."

"Are you kidding?" Kyle answered obviously excited. "You bet!"

"After all it's not like we have anything else to do, oh yeah, except starting school," I said mostly just to needle Kyle, as I had no issues with extending our time at Spyrius. Kyle thought I was serious, which was half the fun.

"Josh, come on. We don't even know how we are going to get home. We can miss a few days. Plus I'll learn much more with Dan here then I will ever learn in class," he said pleadingly.

"I'm just kidding Kyle. Just giving you a hard time, we can stay for a bit."

He did bring up a good point though; I had no idea how we were going to get home. We couldn't go back through Oz since Larry had taken the liberty of smashing the projector at Virginia Tech. Also at some point my parents were going to call me for an update on how things we going. Not sure how they would take if I told them I was 3,000 miles away. At this point though I was too tired to think about it.

"I need to get a few things from my office before we call it a night. Josh, Kyle, want to see my office?"

We accepted and Darlene tagged along, enjoying her time with Kyle who was slowly warming to the idea of Darlene's fondness. We went back to the main Oz control room, now empty, to a door in the back that led to a private elevator that went directly to Sebastian's office.

"It stops here, on the first floor, and at my office on the twelfth floor, which is the top."

We went up and indeed Sebastian had an office at the top that would befit the multi-millionaire owner and CEO of Spyrius. The office was huge with a wall of glass windows that looked out to the lights of the Town of Moses Lake in the distance below. A set of double glass doors led to an area out front where I assume Sebastian's assistants sat, and past them to what looked to be the main elevator area. The elevator we came up in resided in Sebastian's office proper.

We hung around for a little while, Sebastian was having fun showing things off to someone new. Sebastian said he just wanted to check on a few things and then we would figure out what Kyle and I would do for the night.

"Kyle, while we are waiting come downstairs. I'll show you the Oz Creation program real quick," Darlene said directly to Kyle.

"Josh, you want to see the Creation program?"

I could only sigh at Kyle. Ever since Darlene first mentioned that she thought Kyle was cute when we very first met her it was obvious that Darlene wanted to get a little time alone with him. While Kyle was getting a little more comfortable with this he was totally clueless as to Darlene's intent here. I was going to give some excuse as to why they should go together alone, but Sebastian beat me to the punch.

"You two go ahead, there's a few things I still want to discuss with Josh."

Darlene smiled knowing that Sebastian did that just so she could go off with Kyle. As for Kyle, he didn't put up any fuss, which I took as a good sign. Sebastian and I stayed silent while they left out of the office.

Once out of earshot I asked, "So was there something you actually wanted to talk to me about, or what that totally an excuse to get Kyle and Darlene alone?"

"Your friend is a little…" he paused, trying to find words to not possibly offend me.

"Socially awkward?" I finished.

"I was actually about to say clueless!" he said with a laugh.

"Seriously," Sebastian continued, "I did want to ask you one thing."

"What?"

"So I know Kyle can pick locks real good, or so I was told, but how good of programmer and hacker is he? Or I will rephrase it, how passionate of a programmer is he when he's working on something he cares about?"

That took me by surprise and a bunch of things ran through my mind real fast. Was he just making casual talk? Or was he asking because he was seeing if Kyle would be interested in a job? After all he did need a new programmer to replace Cho, and it seemed they needed someone with a computer forensics background. Actually Kyle might be a good fit, and he already knew about the Oz project, but then how would I feel? Ironically I was thrilled the idea of Darlene being interested in Kyle, but the idea of Kyle suddenly taking a job some 3,000 miles away was not something I particularly relished. I knew that his dad would be all for it, but I wasn't sure if I wanted to make Kyle sound too good.

"Uh, why do you ask?" I said hesitantly.

"Just interested."

And then he just stopped, waiting for me to respond, making me feel uncomfortable. "I mean, he's a good programmer."

"I don't care about good, what about passion?"

"Uh, I really don't know. I guess it depends if it's something he's passionate about."

"I mean I do need another programmer eventually, and I could use a forensics expert… But enough of that, you are obviously uncomfortable about that, which I find interesting. No, I have a much more serious question for you. I want your opinion of what to do with Randy."

"What do you mean?"

"I mean the moral, ethical and practical situation we are in. What do we do with him? Do we just let him sit in that room until he dies? Is that morally and ethically correct? He was obviously willing to kill all of us and sell the Oz technology to someone who might use it to wage war and kill millions, but do we stand as judge and jury? On the other hand, what if we take him out and turn him in? It would expose the whole Oz program at a time when it is still in its infancy. What would be the consequences of that?" Then he stood up and looked straight at me, "Joshua Amandil, what would you do if you were in my situation and had to make that decision?"

Wow, did this guy know how to put people in uncomfortable positions. To be honest I was so concerned about being in the moment that I never even thought of the long-term implications of what had happened.

"Why me, I'm just a college kid you barely know?"

"That's a cop out and you know it. I hate wishy-washy people, and you're not stupid, so answer my questions now."

He said that not in a mean way, but with a very authoritative presence. Though he did sit back down which took a little edge off of his posture. I got the feeling I was not going to get out of this without giving some sort of educated response. I think he was looking for someone to challenge him. So I took a deep breath and tried to do just that.

"Okay. Let's look at the last point first. How long do you think you are really going to keep this a secret? I mean you just let four unknown college kids roam around in here. You have, what, two dozen people who are working on this project and you already found a handful willing to sell it to the highest bidder. Even if not for nefarious purposes someone is just going to tell someone else."

"Yes, true, good points. And yes, I made an obvious mistake in letting you all in, from that angle only. Obviously it turned out to be a very good thing, as I never would have found out Randy's plans without you! But look at the Manhattan Project. That was kept secret for years with far more people."

"True, but that was different."

"How?"

"It was a different era for one, where it was easier to contain and isolate people and data. Also they were developing the atomic bomb to stop the evil Nazi empire, which was a real threat to humanity, so it bonded the people together more. This project is more esoteric. It may have great applications for mankind but no one really knows what. It's not being developed to counter an immediate threat. Lastly there are your security protocols. They may be good, but you stuck a working projector in an apartment in Blacksburg, VA. I don't think the atomic bomb plans were ever left in a college dorm."

"Fair points, but what does that have to do with Randy?"

"It makes less attractive the case that we, you, have the right to decide Randy's fate because the risk of exposing the Oz project outweighs the negatives of going against the societal norms of due process that we all subscribe to in this country."

He was about to say something, but I was on a roll now. "And what about myself, Kyle, Darlene and Dan? What if any one of us was uncomfortable with a decision to just leave Randy there? Do you have the right to force us to go along? It's not like we could just vote on it, what if the losers don't want to go along?"

"No, you are right, it would have to be a consensus. Voting is a horrible way to decide things by the way. It's only one step removed from a dictatorial decree, as you will almost always have someone disenfranchised."

"And you haven't even touched on Cho. What are you going to do with him, just throw his body in and incinerator? And that Bradley guy? He's been into Oz. Do we even know where he is? And for that matter what about the unknown programmer who was helping Randy? You have so many loose ends. But I do agree with you on one thing, whatever the decision would be it should be a consensus. You may have more weight, but all of us who were involved in this should have input, because it affects all of us. But it's not a decision I could make right here on the spot."

"Very good. I'm not too worried about Bradley right now because..."

And that is as far as he got. From the corner of Sebastian's office we both heard a ding. The ding of an elevator when it reaches its destination. I turned towards the elevator that we had come up in barely ten minutes earlier and saw the light indicating someone reaching this floor. Sebastian noticed it too and he looked very puzzled at who could possibly be using his private elevator. I didn't have time to ask Sebastian about it, because the door opened and out stepped Randy. He did not look like he was trapped in a room in Oz, he looked very real, very angry, and carried yet another very substantial gun.

"Keep your hands where I can see them or I will blow your head off," he said with authority as he pointed the gun straight at Sebastian. "Whatever you are looking for, it will do you no good anyway."

I was frozen, not knowing what to do. It was Sunday night, the top floor of an empty building and there was no one to help us.

"And you again," he said pointing the gun at me. "How convenient for you to be here, though your little friend seems to be missing. Have you ever watched Scooby-Doo?"

I wasn't sure what to say at that question which seemed out of left field.

"I said, HAVE YOU EVER WATCHED SCOOBY-DOO?"

That was said with force and a look of madness in his eyes. I didn't think it wise to ignore him.

"Yes of course," I said trying to be as calm as possible.

"Keep your hands where I can see them," he quickly looked back at Sebastian behind his desk. At this point he was standing slightly to the side of the desk, myself in front. He was only a couple of feet from both Sebastian and I.

"At the end of Scooby-Doo," he continued looking back at me, "the captured bad guy would always say how he would have gotten away with everything if it wasn't for those meddling kids. Well, I would have gotten away with it all if it wasn't for YOU meddling kids."

He said the last with definite spite and at this point, once again, I was really scared.

"Yes, if it wasn't for you I could have sold this whole Oz thing for hundreds of millions of dollars. Not a million, not tens of millions, but hundreds. Enough so that I could buy an airplane and a private island just like you," he said turning back to Sebastian.

"Randy, you know I don't have a private island," Sebastian said, though I am not sure why as it just seemed to enrage Randy even more.

"Whatever. The point is I finally could have had what you have. And I would have earned it, unlike you who just suckled on your daddy's money."

I have no idea what that actually meant, but it was obvious that he had some long seated jealousy of Sebastian's wealth. I didn't need my semester of psychology to figure that one out. What I didn't know was how he was here. After all it was only a few minutes ago that Dan had said that he was still trapped in that room that Kyle and I were in with no way out. He seemed to have read my mind on that one.

"Oh, I bet your wondering how I got out of that little trap you and Danny Boy set up for me. Well let me tell you something, do you think Cho was the only one on my side? There are others Sebastian. Waive a couple of million dollars under the noses of some people and you can get them to do an awful lot. Not everyone is so filthy rich that they can afford to be all altruistic all the time."

"Who..." Sebastian barely got out before Randy interrupted him.

"You think I am going to tell you. HA! That person did a good job though, wish I could reward that person, but I feel it's probably too late now. Maybe it's too late, I don't know, maybe I can still pull this off though things haven't been going to plan. You know, I tried to reason with you at dinner, giving you a chance to come aboard and join me. But you would have none of it. But no issues, I was going to put into motion plan B where all of you would be trapped in a special room in Oz that you could never get out of. Then all of you would just cleanly disappear off the face of the Earth. The police could look all they wanted to, they would never find anything. I will tell you this though, if I can't have my wealth, then I'm going to take you down with me too. I've spent the last three years kissing your ass, waiting for my chance to finally get my payday and if I can't have it then you're not going to enjoy it either."

He said the last line very slowly and deliberately. At this point Randy seemed like a bomb ready to go off. He was a cornered rat and he saw no foreseeable way out.

"Randy, look at me," Sebastian said. "It doesn't have to end like this. We can talk this over and come up…"

"Shut up. Your time is through. I'm going to take this place down, starting with you."

And for the second time in only few hours I heard the concussive sound of a gun being fired.

Chapter 16

Randy faced Sebastian and fired from only a few feet away. The sound was again deafening and I felt the shockwave like before. The whole world around me seemed to slip into slow motion as I saw the bullet hit Sebastian right in his chest. It knocked him back in his chair and he started tumbling backwards toward the floor. That's all I noticed as my conscious mind seemed to be frozen in place. Then some deep primordial part of my brain in charge of flight or fight response kicked in and I felt my legs turn and start running out the door.

I made it as far as the double glass doors of Sebastian's office proper, and just as I was pushing the left door open I heard what sounded like another cannon blast. I must have winced, awaiting the shock of a bullet entering me. But instead the glass of the right door shattered in an explosion like fireworks on the Fourth of July as the bullet passed through it. It was as if that jolt kicked my brain out of the slow motion state, suddenly everything was back in real time. I saw the exit sign to the stairs to the right in the administrative area and made a beeline towards them. Maybe the elevator lobby would have been the better choice? Probably not, I don't know, but I was in no position to second-guess myself.

The gun fired again as I was racing for the stair doors. I vaguely remembered seeing something on TV about how difficult it actually was to hit someone running when firing a handgun. One of those shows debunking TV shows and movies where the good guy always seems to hit the bad guy even though they are both running at full speed. I don't know why I remembered that, but I certainly hoped it was true.

I pushed the door to the stairs open and heard another shot. This time I felt something. I was not sure what or even where, just something.

I had no time to analyze the situation as I turned, faced the stairs and jumped, grabbing the railing on the way and swinging myself down taking the whole first section of stairs in one bound, hitting the landing between floors with considerable force. If it hurt, I did not know. The adrenaline pumping through me at this point masked any pain or any other feeling I might have had at that time. I grabbed the next railing and repeated the same exploit, ending up on the landing to the floor below. I heard another shot, echoing in the stairwell, but seemingly farther away. Here I thought I had an advantage. Randy could not use both hands to propel himself down the stairs like I did and still hold on to the gun. So he had to run down the stairs. Probably taking a few at a time, but definitely slower.

After repeating a few floors I could tell that I was creating definite space between Randy and me. There were no more shots and I assumed he realized that he could not hit me. I started realizing I did have real pain, though I still was not sure where. I think it was in my legs, but it seemed somewhere else as well. My mind flipped for a second to Sebastian. He was shot in the chest at almost point blank range by what was obviously a decent caliber gun. I had to assume he was dead.

After two more floors the sign on the door said seven. I had gone down five floors on pure adrenaline and it suddenly all caught up to me. A feeling of sudden exhaustion washed over me and I had to stop for a second. I realized that I was in pain, my shoulder and my shins hurt. My chest was tight from the stress and my ears were ringing like I had just spent the last hour at a rock concert. Through the ringing I became aware of a door closing far above me, and then silence. Randy had stopped following me, probably realizing he was not going to catch me, and exited the stairs at some floor. I did not know if he went back up to the twelfth or exited on another floor, either way, an immense feeling of relief washed over me.

That feeling lasted only for a brief second and I was suddenly terrified again. There were guards on the first floor, but it was Sunday, and there were only three that I saw. They were armed, but if Randy got to them first he would have the element of total surprise. I needed to get down to them before Randy could get an elevator and get down there. I was running down the stairs, taking two to three steps at a time, using the railing to stop from falling. I was in pain, I couldn't even see fully straight, but I just kept going. Somewhere along my trek I became aware of alarm bells going off. Someone had triggered some sort of alarm, though I did not know from whom. It seemed like hours had gone by even though it was probably less than a minute when I pushed open the first floor door into the main lobby.

One of the guards turned and looked toward me, his gun already drawn. Of course, they heard the shots and probably turned on the alarm. They assumed I might be a threat, who knew what I looked like at that time.

"Randy, he has a gun, he shot Sebastian."

And then I collapsed to the floor. I kept repeating that Randy had a gun and beware of Randy, but things became a blur as the adrenaline that was sustaining me stopped flowing. Then I really thought I was losing it as I heard a voice.

"It's Randy, he's armed and will kill and I have no idea where he is."

I heard someone yell out, "He's in Sebastian's office", but I was more intrigued by who had just talked before. I looked around and saw Sebastian walking from the hallway toward the lobby, obviously in pain. He was clutching his bleeding chest, though not with anywhere near the amount of blood I would have expected. He also had a gun in his other hand, which I first thought was odd until I remembered he took Randy's original gun from Pullman up with him to his office. I shook my head to try to clear the cobwebs out, but it was no illusion, Sebastian was somehow alive. The man who had just spoke continued.

"You two lock the elevators and go up to the twelfth. I'll stay here with these two, police should be here soon, I'll get an ambulance."

Sebastian slumped to the ground against to the guard station not far from me. "I locked my elevator so he can't use that. Keep your eye on the stairs though, he may come out here," He said to the security guard.

"He's still in your office, he looks like he's destroying the place," the guard said to Sebastian obviously looking at a monitor that was out of my field of view."

Sebastian turned and looked at me. "Josh, are you okay?"

"I guess, I don't know," was all I could get out.

"You've been shot."

I had? If so, I was not sure where. My shoulder still hurt, as did my shins, but I didn't see any blood. Oddly all I could say in response was, "So have you."

At that moment I could hear a door open and running from the other hallway where the stairs led down to the basement housing the Oz project. Dan came into view first, followed by Kyle and Darlene.

"What's the alarm…?" But that's as far as he got before he noticed both Sebastian and myself on the floor.

A few expletives came out of Dan's mouth as he rushed over to Sebastian.

"Take this gun Dan and help Dominick in case Randy comes down the stairs,"

"Randy!" Dan exclaimed. "What, he can't be here."

"I wasn't shot by Mickey Mouse, just do it," Sebastian said with force and Dan complied.

Meanwhile Kyle had arrived at my side, looking more panic-stricken than I was. He kept asking me if I was okay, and I was just ignoring him. I was not sure if I could take his hysteria. Darlene looked significantly calmer but when she put her hand on the back of my right shoulder a jolt of pain shot through my whole body and I jumped out of my skin, or at least I felt like I did."

"OW! What the, STOP." I got up to my knees and then bent over trying to catch my breath from the pain.

"I'm sorry," Darlene said a few times. "You know you have been shot."

"Where?"

"In the back of your shoulder. You're bleeding, but it doesn't look too bad. It looks like it skimmed the top of your shoulder, but I really can't tell."

"Well it sure hurts."

Looking up I did notice a trail of blood leading from the door to the stairs I came from to where I was. It wasn't too bad of a trail, but I guess I was bleeding. At this point Kyle was kneeling next to me and I put my left arm on him to steady myself. I told them both to shut up so I could catch my breath. I was probably way too curt in my request, but they both obliged and I forced myself to take some long deep breaths and try to relax. The intense pain from Darlene hand has subsided back into dull throbbing that covered my whole body.

Sebastian was still sitting there. He too looked like he was trying to relax. He had taken his hand off his chest, and while I could see a little pool of blood he didn't look too bad. Certainly not the way I expected someone shot at almost point blank range to look. I expected a gaping hole. He saw that I was staring at him and he gave me a thumbs up. Dan and the guard Dominick were discussing things and pointing at what I assume were security monitors. I heard police sirens pull up to the main entrance. I assume Dominick had let them through the security gate.

I'm not quite sure how long I stayed in that position. Everything was tolerable in the position I was in so I didn't want to move. The police were in by now and discussing the situation with Dominick. Soon after I could hear some back and forth with Dominick over the two-way radio he had, probably to the other two guards that went upstairs. Shortly after that he turned to Sebastian.

"Randy fired at them and they fired back. Randy's dead, Nicole and Christopher are fine. I'm sorry."

Sebastian just shook his head in acknowledgement. I'm not really sure why the Dominick guy said he was sorry. Maybe because he knew Sebastian had been close to Randy and didn't understand what was going on and why Randy suddenly turned into a madman with a gun shooting people. I assumed Nicole and Christopher were the other two guards, so that was good news.

With the immediate threat gone Dan went to sit next to Sebastian to see how he was doing. Darlene also migrated over to check on him. Kyle was still steadying me and I realized he hadn't said a word since I told him to shut up which made me feel a little guilty.

"Sorry Kyle, didn't mean to yell at you."

"It's okay," he said and smiled at me. That made me feel a little better.

An ambulance pulled up and some paramedics came in. They went straight for Sebastian. I'm sure the paramedics were told who had been shot and considering Sebastian's stature in the town I don't blame them.

But he, who seemed a little more chipper than before, waived them over and told them to take care of me first, which they did. They cut most of my shirt off, poked a bit causing me to scream again and started to clean me up. At this point they realized I was not in immediate danger and two of the three paramedics went back to Sebastian. The conclusion for me was that it was mostly a flesh wound, but the bullet probably nicked the top of my scapula (or shoulder bone) and that was what was causing my pain. They would need to take x-rays to be sure. As for my legs, the paramedic pulled my pants legs up and concluded I might have a bruised tibia (my shin bone). It probably happened at some point when I was leaping down the stairs.

The paramedics had Sebastian's shirt and undershirt off at this point and were poking and prodding him in the chest. Darlene came back and I had to ask her the question that was bugging me most of all.

"Darlene, I saw Sebastian shot in the chest at almost point blank range. It had enough force to knock him clear off his chair. How the heck is he still alive?"

Darlene looked at me a bit puzzled, but Sebastian heard what I said.

"Would you rather I have a massive hole in my chest?" he called over to me.

"Umm, no, of course not," I called back rather embarrassed.

"Relax, I am just giving you a hard time. See this," he said as he picked up his undershirt, which did look a bit thicker and heavier than a regular undershirt. He winced in pain a bit as he picked it up and quickly let go. One of the paramedics admonished him for picking it up. "It's a lightweight, bullet resistant undershirt. Latest technology and all the range for billionaire executives," he said with a little self-mockery and exaggeration. I didn't think Sebastian's personal net worth actually reached into the billions as most of his inheritance was tied up in Spyrius and Oz.

"All the protection of a bullet proof vest without all the bulk. Costs a bloody fortune, let me tell you, and I don't think it works quite as well as a bullet proof vest as the bullet did sort of go through, and it seems I might have a broken sternum. But all things considered, I'll take it."

"And you just happen to be wearing it today?"

"I have several, and I wear them most days actually. Believe it or not I actually get death threats every so often. You never know when some crazed person is going to try to take a pot shot at you. Never expected it would be someone I thought was a close friend…"

He kind of trailed off with that and I let it go. Both Sebastian and I needed to go to the hospital to get some x-rays at that point anyway. Sebastian was able to walk to the ambulance under his own power. As for me, I was helped by one of the technicians and Dan so I wasn't putting all my weight on my legs.

Sitting in an ambulance in a bit of pain having been through a major ordeal, one tends to revert back to his base instincts. I wanted my mommy. I may be eighteen and technically an adult, but at this moment I just wanted to lean on my mom and have her hold me and tell me everything was going to be okay. Alas she was 3,000 miles away, as far away from my mom as I have ever been in my life. So Kyle sat next to me. Not even close to the same but it would have to do, and having a friendly face there was far better than having none at all. I was cold, tired and exhausted. It had been a very long day. Sebastian sat across and looked pretty tired too. Dan followed in Sebastian's fancy electric sports car, and Darlene followed in her car.

When we arrived at the hospital Sebastian suggested that Dan and Darlene go home, in fact he ordered them too. No one was dying, and even with a broken sternum he would be able to drive just fine.

Everyone would meet tomorrow at 9:00 in the morning to figure things out. So they both wished us all well. Darlene gave Sebastian a quick hug, came over to me and did the same, saying she was happy that I was okay, then went over to Kyle and said she was glad he was okay too and gave him a little peck on the cheek. Kyle said nothing, though his turning a bright shade of red said it all. I was not the least bit upset at the fact that Darlene obviously thought Kyle was adorable, but hey, I was the one that was shot not Kyle! Either way both Dan and her left in Darlene's car.

Emergency rooms always seem to take forever. Thankfully it was a fairly quiet night, but we were not dying so neither Sebastian nor myself were a high priority. I thought Sebastian's status in town might help out, and maybe it actually did but it still took an hour just to get x-rays. While waiting for the doctor Sebastian got in touch with his model girlfriend Anya, who was in Milan, Italy at the time doing some model thing, to let her know he was fine just in case there were any news reports about a shooting at Spyrius. I thought about calling my parents, but I didn't want to have to deal with all the questions like, what was I doing in the state of Washington. I'd figure out something to tell them later. Thankfully I wasn't in such bad shape that they would have called my parents, my insurance is through them so the hospital had their contact information. That would have been difficult to explain. As for Kyle, I doubt calling his parents even crossed his mind.

Kyle and I had plenty of things still to ask Sebastian about as we waited, and there were plenty of loose ends still to figure out, but I didn't feel like thinking, much less talking, and I don't think Sebastian did either.

Eventually the doctor came, she was a nice middle aged woman. She knew who Sebastian was but didn't care or seem particularly impressed. She had a very matter of fact attitude, which was fine with me.

Sebastian's sternum was only bruised and that really was the extent of his injuries. Pretty lucky I thought. Nothing to do for a bruised sternum but to rest and let it heal on its own.

As for me, the bullet just barely nicked my scapula resulting in a hairline fracture that was barely visible on the x-ray. So small I couldn't see it even when the doctor was pointing right at it on the x-ray. She said that hairline fractures were actually more painful than a clean break some of the time and that there was nothing for them to fix. I just had to let it heal naturally. They put my arm in a sling which would be there for the next six weeks or so which I felt would be quite annoying. Nothing was broken with my shins, but I had some minor bruising on both. Rest and ice was her recommendation. They had wrapped some cold packs around them when we first came in which I ended up taking with me. She said not to walk too much and stay off my feet if I started feeling pain.

By this time it was 1:00 in the morning, which for Kyle and I was 4:00 in the morning Eastern Time. True, for a college student staying up to four in the morning is not that big of a deal, but normally one does not have a day like we had. We started in Roanoke at 8:30 that morning, even though that seemed like a week ago, went into Oz, had some madmen chase us, hung out outside of Los Angeles, went back into Oz, got stuck in an undescriptive room for four hours, came up to Spyrius headquarters, drove to Pullman, had an adventure there with some shooting, back to Spyrius, then more shooting (this time directly at me), and then finally some time in the hospital.

"What do you two want to do?" Sebastian asked. "Obviously you two are staying here for the night. I can take you to a hotel and put you up, or you can spend the night at my place. I have two guest bedrooms and my place overlooks the lake."

To be honest I hadn't put any thought into where to sleep for the night. So much was going on that where I was going to sleep had yet to cross my mind.

"Your place," Kyle said sounding a little excited.

"Fine with me," I said, trying to sound a little more restrained, though to be honest I thought it would be pretty cool to see a multi-millionaires place.

We walked out to Sebastian's car. I did fine, my legs did feel a bit better after being on ice for an hour. Sebastian's $100,000 plus electric sports car was impressive, and if I wasn't so exhausted I would have probably appreciated it more. Sebastian said it would only be a fifteen minute drive to his place.

"So Kyle," Sebastian said as we drove, "how good a programmer slash hacker are you anyway?"

Why was he asking this now I thought?

"Well, pretty good, I think at least. I wrote a custom database system for my friend's dad's company when I was fifteen, and Josh and I wrote a shareware game that we make a little money on, and I breadboarded, built, and programmed my own robot for a senior class project, won a few hacking contests at DefCon, both the kids ones *and* the adult ones, oh and I got straight A's in my computer science classes at school last year, though that was not too hard. Why?"

"Well with Cho out of the picture I do need another programmer and we need someone with some forensics knowledge. Obviously you would need to go through the whole interview process, but would you be interested?"

"Are you serious?" Kyle asked with obvious enthusiasm.

"Well we would need a resume, you would have to pass and interview by myself and Dan, but yes I am serious."

"Oh course, absolutely," he said fully awake now. But then he looked at me and came back to reality. "I'll have to think about it first," he noted backing himself up a little.

"Well you can let me know tomorrow. I figured you would have to run it by your dad, or others."

He said the last part with a little emphasis. I purposely didn't say a thing, or even give Kyle a hint of what I was thinking. I am not sure what Sebastian was doing bringing this up now, but I knew he was doing it on purpose. A continuation of what he was asking me earlier. To be honest I now wasn't sure if Sebastian was the cool, multi-millionaire tech mogul I thought at first, or if he was just a jerk.

His house was on the end of a peninsula overlooking the water. It was gated and very nice, but not anywhere near as big as I thought it would be. It wasn't small, and this was obviously the very upscale part of town, but not a huge mansion like I envisioned. Then again this area wasn't the French Rivera with tons of millionaires and movie stars. Nor was this Sebastian's only place. I knew he had a place in L.A, and he still had the family mansion somewhere in Texas, and I could see him having some vacation homes too.

Inside it was brand new and immaculate. It looked like it was built new when Sebastian moved Spyrius here and had all the most expensive finishes and latest gadgets. Sebastian had a live in housekeeper, Barbara, who looked like a typical Asian mother. He had called her when we said we would stay to get the rooms ready and obviously mentioned that he was in the hospital. Not sure how much more she knew, but she went and doted over him asking if he was alright and what she could do. I really didn't care. I just wanted to get to bed and actually interrupted and asked such. Barbara showed me my room and where the bathroom was and after using the latter I went into the former, stripped to my boxer briefs and collapsed into bed. I'm not even sure what Kyle was doing and I didn't care. I was asleep before my head fully sunk into the very soft and luxurious pillow.

Chapter 17

I awoke to sun pouring in through a pair of very large windows in my room. I moved to sit up and noticed distinct pain in my shoulder from stiffness. My legs felt pretty well though, only a mild, dull pain. I got up and walked over to the window and looked out. It was a pretty incredible view overlooking the river inlet forking off Moses Lake itself into downtown. There was a dock below and a descent sized speedboat which I was sure was Sebastian's. If this was the view from the guest bedroom I could only imagine what the master was like.

"You got the good room, mine is on the other side and overlooks the road."

"Jesus!" I exclaimed turning to face Kyle who was relaxing in a very comfortable looking chair. "Don't scare me like that."

It didn't bother me that I was wearing nothing but my boxer briefs, and my sling. Kyle stayed overnight enough in my room that he was like a brother in that aspect. Plus he was sitting there in only his skivvies, he preferred briefs for some reason, and a T-shirt I had never seen before.

"What time is it, and what are you doing here?" I asked.

"Sorry, I didn't think I needed to ask permission."

"Stop it, that's not what I meant. I meant why are you just sitting here?"

"It's a quarter to seven. Remember it's almost ten o'clock our time. I got up about a half hour ago and knew I wasn't going to get back to sleep, so I came in here to see what you were up to, I mean I didn't want to go walking around the house. After I noticed the view you have I just sat in this chair and watched the sun rise. Figured I would just wait until you got up, you needed the rest after what you went through last night. Pretty incredible view, huh?"

I agreed.

"There's a new shirt and sweater for you there, I got this clean T-shirt. Barbara put them in last night before we all went to bed. You were sound asleep."

I was glad to see that. My original shirt had been cut off by the paramedics, and I left the hospital still wearing the hospital gown as a shirt. "How late did you all stay up?"

"Not very, I probably went to bed fifteen minutes after you. I may not have been shot, but I was pretty out of it too."

I sat down in another chair, not wanting to stand on my feet longer than necessary. Kyle continued with a much softer tone.

"Speaking of being shot. Well, umm, when Dan, Darlene and I rounded the corner and the alarms were blaring, I had no idea what was going on, but when I saw you lying there with a trail of blood behind you, I…"

He paused for a second and was actually getting choked up. I didn't want to put him through that so I interrupted him.

"Kyle, I get it, and I appreciate it, but I am fine. So don't worry, everything turned out fine."

"No Josh, you don't quite get it. I'm in a bit of a quandary now."

"Why?"

"Well before I went to bed I was getting something to drink in the kitchen and Sebastian asked me if I was really interested in a job even though it was just me and not you that he wanted to hire."

Ouch I thought. I wasn't really sure about what my feelings were about my best friend moving as far across country as you can get, but what I was sure of was that I didn't at all like the way Sebastian was going about it. Regardless I had to take the high road.

"Come on Kyle, I would never stand in the way of you taking your dream job."

"And Sebastian thought it would be good for Darlene too, having someone else her age around. And if you hadn't noticed I think she kind of likes me a bit."

"No, really? I hadn't noticed at all," I said dripping with as much sarcasm as possible.

"But that's not fair. How do I choose between a cool job and, well, a kind of cute girl who seems to like me, and my best friend? It's just not fair. Well maybe I'll end up blowing the interview and it will be all for naught anyway."

"You know Kyle, no one said life was fair. But we'll figure it out. But don't worry about it this second, let's go downstairs and check this place out."

I got dressed, Kyle went back to his room and did the same, and we both went down to the main level.

Seen in the daylight and not being half asleep I could really take in the place. There was one great room with the kitchen off to the side. The ceilings were two stories high with a wall of glass windows looking out to the backyard which gradually sloped down to the water and dock below. Everything was high end, from the TV that must have been eighty inches across to the crown molding, works of art, gleaming new appliances and marble counter tops. This was the kind of house you see in those architecture magazines, but to be honest, I was kind of hungry.

"Do you really think you should be going through his refrigerator?" Kyle asked me as I took out some eggs, cheese, cherry tomatoes and an onion. I may not be as good a cook as Larry, but could make an omelet if necessary.

"What's he going to do, throw us out of the house?"

"He might get mad if we just help ourselves to his food."

I thought for a second that Kyle might be worried that Sebastian would not offer him a job because we cooked some of his food. Or worse that he thought I was doing it on purpose to sabotage him.

"Kyle, we are his guests and he knows all the proper social graces. He will not get mad at us for cooking some eggs. We'll make enough for him too."

"Are you sure?"

"Yes."

And so I found a skillet, figured out the restaurant quality gas stove that was built like a tank and cooked an omelet. It was a little more difficult with the use of one and a half hands, but I managed. I had Kyle toast up some bread to keep him busy.

"I hope your making some for me," called Sebastian from above.

He was watching us from the upstairs railing overlooking the whole downstairs area. Who knows how long he was sitting there, but he was wearing a robe and what looked like silk pajamas underneath. I thought it looked fairly ridiculous.

"I told Barbara she didn't have to get up to make us breakfast since she was supposed to be off yesterday."

"There is plenty for you," I responded curtly.

"I wasn't sure if it was okay to just cook your food," Kyle said almost apologetically, which annoyed me a bit.

"I heard Kyle, no problem."

He came down and the three of us ate breakfast. I remarked that he looked like Hugh Hefner, which he not only seemed to find genuinely funny but also seemed amused that an eighteen year old knew who Hugh Hefner was. Chatting during breakfast was kept light, Sebastian mentioned nothing about the events of yesterday, probably waiting until we were all together at Spyrius, and made no mention of a job for Kyle.

After breakfast he got some towels for Kyle and me and while he took a shower in the master bath, Kyle and I took turns in the guest bathroom. After that we still had an hour to kill, and Sebastian showed us how to work his media center in the family room so we could watch TV. I think he was going to sit down and talk with us, but by this time his phone started ringing non-stop. News of a shooting at Spyrius headquarters and the fact that Sebastian had been shot had gotten out and was all over the Internet. He was fielding calls from friends, co-workers, news organizations, his agent, stockbroker and anyone else you can think of. The police also called, needless to say they wanted a full interview with not only Sebastian, but all of us. They weren't pushing too hard though as they were there yesterday to see the shootout with Randy and the two guards in person.

I took this time to call Sylvia, mostly to tell her that Sebastian mentioned that he called off any switching of apartments for the moment, so they did not need to worry about that. That Evan Duncan guy who was going to work on agriculture in Oz would just have to wait, but at some point they probably would have to switch. She seemed fine with that. I also wanted to know how Larry and her were doing. She said okay for now, they were busy with the start of school. She had not heard about the shooting at Spyrius, and I didn't feel like bringing it up so I just told here that Kyle and I were doing well and were not sure when we would be back. Lastly I told her that I promised Sebastian that they would not say anything about Oz to anyone, something I told him on the ride home. She said not to worry, Larry was too freaked out about it to tell anyone and she would keep it a secret.

I also texted my mom. Told her that I was just checking in, everything was going fine and I would call her over the weekend. Since she had no idea where I was texting from I hoped that would hold my parents off for a while. I asked Kyle if he wanted to do the same with his parents and he just shrugged. I think I could count on one hand all the times his parents called him during all of last year, so I didn't think he was worried about it.

Finally around 8:30 or so Sebastian had enough of all the calls and told us he was ready to go. He did have one line of questioning for us as we were leaving.

"By the way, the two of you feel normal, right? I mean separate from you injuries Josh."

"Yes, I guess," Kyle answered not sure why he was asking the question.

"Why?" I asked.

"Oh, nothing."

I stared at him. Yet another thing to find slightly annoying about Sebastian.

"Okay, it's just that when you went through the door, um, portal at Harvey Mudd that was the first time someone went out a door that didn't have a copy of their specific material. We had been doing tests with cats, dogs and even a monkey, with no ill effects, but never a human."

"Great," I said sarcastically.

"Yeah, Darlene mentioned something about that," Kyle added.

"Like I said, with our testing we were, well are, 99.999 percent sure it would work fine as the genetic material that makes us up is all the same and the Oz program has your specific makeup that would use that material. Not much we can do about it now, but you two can go down as pioneers in testing Oz!"

He said the last part with a bit of a forced smile, like that should make us feel better. But he was right, there was nothing we could do about it now, and I did feel the same as always. So I decided not to worry about it.

"And the Vaughn's, who originally went in at Harvey Mudd came out here in that sub-basement where a copy was made of their genetic makeup already, so they weren't doing what we did," Kyle stated to make sure he had everything straight.

"You got it Kyle."

And with that we headed down to Spyrius.

Chapter 18

This time I got to admire Sebastian's electric sports car a little more as I was awake and sitting in the passenger seat. I felt like I was in a jet fighter and Sebastian had a little fun showing off the pure torque of the electric motor, going from zero to sixty miles per hour in something like four seconds. Being a multi-millionaire did have its perks.

Coming up to Spyrius as a passenger in a car instead of leaving as a patient in an ambulance, I was actually able to see what it looked like. Yes there was a big fence with barbed wire on the top and a big gate with a few guard stations, but the building did not seem anything prison like. I guess the reports were exaggerated. I seemed like a normal twelve story office building. Pretty non-descript, but Sebastian probably didn't want to call too much attention to it.

It was a Monday, the week before the Labor Day holiday weekend, so the normal stream of workers were parading in. Many people were milling about outside, probably discussing whatever rumors there were about what happened the night before. A few police cars were parked inside the gate and the local news truck was parked right outside of it.

Sebastian thanked the numerous well-wishers as we went in, but otherwise funneled Kyle and I quickly in to his private elevator and up to his private office. He left a note for Dan and Darlene to come up as soon as they came in but otherwise was not to be bothered. Dan and Darlene each arrived only a few minutes behind us and the five of us went into a conference room off of the room where Sebastian's two assistants sat. The conference room was soundproof and had no windows or cameras so we could talk freely.

"What a morning," Dan said. "I think I got twenty calls asking what happened and if you were okay."

"Yes, it's been crazy," Sebastian replied. "But the five of us here are the only five who know the whole story of what happened. We need to figure out what we are going to do about certain things, not the least of which is getting Cho, as well as figure out what we will tell the police. Damn it Dan, I totally didn't think of it, but we can't have anyone going into Oz this morning."

"Already thought of that. I locked the whole thing down when I got home last night. Nobody can get in."

"Well, alright, thinking ahead. That's why I pay you the big bucks," he said with a little humor in his voice. "Okay, Josh and I were starting to discuss some of these things before we were so rudely interrupted by Randy. So Josh, why don't you take the lead and start us off?"

"Huh?" was all I could muster out after being taken totally by surprise.

"There's a whiteboard there, feel free to use it if you want. It's electronic but not connected to anything so you can write whatever you want, there will be no record. There are a lot of loose ends and things that need to be figured out. You lead. Pretend this is your company and you have to clean up this mess. Go for it."

I looked around. Dan had the same look as Sebastian, kind of a, 'we don't have all day so get started' look. Darlene was trying to hold back a smile, as if she had a sense of what was going on. Kyle just looked like he was very relieved that it wasn't him that Sebastian called on. I knew that once again Sebastian was doing this on purpose, but I didn't know what that purpose was. What I quickly realized was that no one was going to let me off the hook, and while I was under no actual obligation to play along, part of me found this an interesting challenge. So I stood up and walked to the white board and grabbed the special pen for it. Awkwardly writing with my left hand, trying to be a legible as possible as I put some free flowing topics on the board:

- What's the worst case scenario? Have to tell someone about Oz?
- Randy - What to tell the police about what happened?
- Cho - What to do with him?
- Eusebio - What did he know, what to do?
- Bradley - Where is he, what to do?
- Mystery programmer and others helping Randy. How to find? What to do?
- Security practices going forward, what to improve, lessons learned.

When I was done writing I turned around to see if this seemed to be what Sebastian wanted. Dan and he seemed to be showing approval. I sat back down, my legs still sore from leaping down several flights of stairs.

"Pick one and throw out some thoughts," Dan said, who now seemed as interested as Sebastian in having me play this role.

"Alright, I'll start with the one that Sebastian and I were discussing last night that's now much easier. That's Randy. If we are all going to be interviewed by the police on what happened last night we need to figure out what to tell them."

"So what do you propose?" Darlene asked, now also into what I had to say.

"I say we tell them the truth, at least as far as we need to. It's too hard to make up a story and keep it straight among five people. Plus I have some issues with outright lying to the police. We tell them that Randy was trying to sell some new proprietary technology that Spyrius is working on to the highest bidder and when Sebastian found out and confronted him he tried to kill Sebastian and anyone else who found out his plans. They know the story from there."

"Fair enough," Sebastian said. "What if they want to know what the technology is?"

"We tell them it's proprietary."

"I'll gladly sign an NDA," Dan said playing devil's advocate as if he was the police. I had no idea what an NDA was and I think Dan and Sebastian picked up on that, but Kyle was eager to add something so he popped in.

"Non-disclosure agreement. My dad signs them all the time. You sign it stating you won't reveal any sensitive information about what you are looking at."

"Hmm. Well in that case you tell them that it's a holographic projection technology. That's not a lie per se. Heck, you can even turn it on and show them the portal. Just don't tell them that you can actually disappear into it!"

They all seemed to be nodding in agreement, so I continued on.

"And that brings me to the first point on the list. What is the worst possible outcome here? I think it would be that someone; head detective, police chief, would actually have to be shown what Oz really is. Have him sign that NDA. Is that so terrible? I mean as Sebastian and I were talking yesterday about how you all let four unknown college students go into Oz, how long is this going to stay secret?"

"We didn't let you into Oz, you figured it out on your own and went in before we could stop you." Sebastian corrected me.

"But you didn't turn off our access after we did that first foray," Kyle stated.

"Yes, I know," Sebastian said. "Curiosity got the best of me and I should not have let you all continue. But as I pointed out before it actually worked out for the best as otherwise Randy's plans would have never been exposed."

"True, but that can go to my last point, lessons learned. If you really want to keep this secret maybe you need to add some more security controls?"

"More controls?" Sebastian asked incredulously. "It was locked in a safe hidden in a fake vent! How was I supposed to know you had an expert lock picker with you?"

Kyle just smiled, for Sebastian was obviously not upset, in fact I think he was impressed that we figured everything out. Sebastian then took over for a moment.

"Alright, very good Josh, that is very reasonable and well thought out. Let's stop with that for right now. Anyone, and that includes you Kyle, additions, criticisms, alternate ideas?"

"I think it's a very good plan, as long as we all keep to that same amount of truth," Dan said. "We aren't being interrogated as a suspect here, they just want to find the truth of what happened. I think we should be okay to say that it was a proprietary holographic projection technology, but point out that it had very valuable uses that could be sold for millions of dollars. I think they might wonder about why Randy went so off the deep end if it was just some minor thing."

"I think I can play up the fact that Randy obviously had a deep seated, long standing jealousy of my family's wealth. That would add into why he snapped so bad, and Josh was there to hear him actually say that."

"I don't think Randy's going to be that much of an issue," Dan continued. "I am far more concerned about what we are going to do with Cho's body. That is a real quandary and we need to figure that out in this meeting because he can't just sit there."

"Agree totally," Sebastian said. "Let's table Randy for the moment. Josh, what are we going to do with Cho?"

I kind of looked at him in a why are you asking me to do this way, but he just sat there waiting for me to say something. I think I would more enjoy this if it was a hypothetical exercise, but it wasn't. A real person was lying dead who had been murdered.

"Fine," I said a little sternly. I turned to write on the board again:

Cho
- Moral questions - Hiding truth of death.
- Legal questions - What do we say happened? Obstructing justice?
- Family - What to do?

"Morally there is theoretically no issue about hiding exactly what happened. He was shot by Randy and Randy is now dead. But my biggest question is what about his family? You can't just hand over the body and say, 'Here's your son, he was killed but we can't tell you how or why?' I think they might call the police on that and then we might have some issues with obstruction of justice. I mean I am sorry, but I don't have an answer here."

"No, that's fine Josh," Dan added in a soothing manner, sensing that I was getting a little tightly wound. "You don't have to have all the answers, you're bringing up great points that we all have to discuss."

"What about Cho's family?" Kyle asked wanting to have some input into this process. "Sebastian, you said he had no family in America, but what about friends, roommates? What about family back in wherever he is from? What do you know?"

"Cho kept mostly to himself and lived alone. I know that much," Darlene answered.

"Cho came from Korea, or so he said." Dan said. "He came to my attention at a recruiting day at Harvey Mudd, even though he never went there, when we first about to move up here. Said he could program and had no issues locating to Moses Lake as he had no family or close friends. He passed all the programming tests fine and we hired him for Spyrius first to see if he would work out. He seemed fine so eventually we migrated him to the Oz project."

"He was an odd one," Sebastian continued. "When we first hired him he didn't put anyone down for an emergency contact or list his parents. He had his green card so that's all we really needed. He got a place here by himself. Never seemed to go out, never really made friends, just did the work asked of him. So I really have no idea who we would contact. Park is a very common last name, as is Cho a common first name. Equivalent of John Smith here. Maybe that should have been a red flag, but there were nothing to indicate he was anything else then just a very quiet young man."

"At least we can remember that at the end he realized what Randy was doing was wrong," Darlene said with a sigh.

"So then what do we do?" Sebastian asked. "There is no way we can bring attention to the authorities without fully explaining Oz. I mean we can't just put his body back in Eusebio's bedroom. Ideas?"

"Does it really matter?" Kyle asked.

We all looked at him to explain.

"I don't mean to sound cold, even though this probably will... But to be logical, if he has no next of kin to contact and no one here that cares, is it worth exposing Oz to a whole bunch of authorities when nothing is really going to come of it? It's a risk based decision. I say we get his phone, which is probably on him, and see if we can locate anyone he called or contacted with on a personal level. If so then we take it from there, if not then let it be."

"Yeah, that's a bit cold," I said to Kyle.

"Looking at his phone is a great idea," Darlene added.

"Cold. That's a great idea!" Dan exclaimed. "Look we already messed with a crime scene as it is, so in for a penny, in for a pound. We can put his body in cold storage. I can create a tiny featureless room, not unlike what Josh and Kyle were in, just the size to house his body. Have it floating outside of Oz proper and kept at a well below freezing temperature. It will be in a kind of suspended animation until we figure out what to do."

Everyone kind of pondered that for a moment before Sebastian spoke.

"That will buy us some time. Let's get his phone, great idea Kyle, put his body in cold storage and take it from there. Anyone disagree?"

Though the whole idea seemed a little sketchy to me, I really couldn't think of a better plan. "I agree, but we should revisit as soon as we see what's in his phone, and maybe from looking in his apartment."

"Okay, we have consensus on that for now. Dan, when we are done here you can get started on that."

"What about our mystery programmer?" Darlene asked

"Dan?" Sebastian asked giving me a reprieve.

"I'll grab Kyle here and we will see what we can find. There are only maybe eight people who even have the accesses to get to the actual core code and are able to do the things that have been done. And no one comes to mind as an obvious possibility. But whoever did this was very clever and covered their tracks well."

"Wait a second," I said. "What about Randy?"

"No way Randy could do this. Oh, I see what you're saying."

"You gave him basically unlimited rights to everything, right?" I asked Sebastian.

He sighed. "Yes, color me stupid. He could have given any single person who works at Spyrius the rights. Randy, Dan and I are the only three people who have rights to everything."

"Any reason he couldn't be using someone outside of Spyrius?" Kyle asked.

Both Sebastian and Dan thought for a moment before Dan answered.

"No. Not really. They could have easily set up a secret VPN or something, creating a protected tunnel allowing full access without any of us knowing. Randy would have no idea how to do that, but if he had someone who did…"

"Great," said Darlene sarcastically. "So we could have a total stranger just lurking around in our code."

"Nothing personal Sebastian," I said. "but I think my last bullet, reviewing your whole security model, is a valid point."

"Kyle and I need to get started on this," Dan said.

"Agreed," Sebastian responded. "Are we all in agreement with what we said earlier about how to respond to the police about the shooting with Randy itself?"

We all nodded.

"Okay, then, Dan and Kyle go get started on rooting this person out, going through Cho's phone and sticking Cho in cold storage. Yes I know this is not ideal, but we will revisit that shortly."

"Get me the phone and I will get everything out of it," Kyle said with confidence.

"Dan, you get that phone by yourself. I don't want anyone else seeing Cho. And nobody goes into Oz until we get Cho moved. Eusebio called me this morning and while I still don't know what he knew I can handle that for now. We cut the head off the dragon so to speak with what happened to Randy, so anyone who was working with him is probably directionless right now."

"What about Bradley?" I asked thinking of the last bullet on my list.

"I asked the guards this morning to pull all his access, so he can't even get on campus. He is a wild card though, but we will have to shelve him for now. Dan, Kyle go. Darlene, help them out. Josh, come with me and let's talk to the police. If we are lucky maybe we can convince them that you and I are all they need to interview."

Chapter 19

Sebastian and I went down to the first floor and found the detectives going through security footage with the security folks. One of the detectives, Vickie, said now would be fine to interview us and that we could be interviewed together. We went back upstairs to Sebastian's office and she started asking questions. It was very informal and we stuck to the script that we had discussed earlier. I didn't say much the whole time.

Sebastian went a lot into the background of his and Randy's friendship to help explain his jealousy and why he did what he did, which I found a bit interesting. Seems they were friends back in Texas where Sebastian grew up with his oil baron father. Randy's family was not poor, actually well off, but nothing like Sebastian's. They were close friends throughout grade school, but by high school they went down different paths. Sebastian was the blue blood rich preppy with excellent grades, whereas Randy started hanging out with the 'wrong' crowd and got into minor trouble. Sebastian went to exclusive Harvey Mudd and then worked at various engineering firms until his father died suddenly, while Randy went to a local college, seemed to get his life together and ended up a security manager for data center. Detectives discovered that he lost a lot of money in bad investments around that time, which Sebastian hadn't known about. Regardless of their different paths, Sebastian and Randy kept in touch informally throughout college, even hanging out occasionally when Sebastian was in Texas. So when Spyrius was started, Randy, with experience as a security manager for a data center, seemed like a natural fit. Sebastian never realized that Randy looked at the position as a chance for financial gain. He was all friendly to Sebastian, almost too friendly, and Sebastian just took it as a reconnection with the grade school friend he once had.

When Vickie was done with the interview she seemed totally satisfied. She saw no reason to interview the others and she already had statements from the three guards on duty last night. We were about to leave when something popped into my head. I didn't have time to ask Sebastian separately, so I just went for it.

"Do you still have Randy's personal belongings?"

"Yes, they are in my car," Vickie responded.

"His cell phone, that's a company phone, right Sebastian?" I asked not having any knowledge if that was the case, but Sebastian picked up on where I was going.

"Yes it is," Sebastian responded. "Can we have that so we can check it to see if he was communicating with anyone else?"

She thought for a second and then said, "If it's a company phone it's your property, and you probably have a better chance of getting into it than we would. Sure, but share any findings related to this case with us."

Sebastian assured her that he would and we went back downstairs. Vickie went out, got the phone and gave it to Sebastian. We went downstairs to the Oz area to see how everyone else was doing.

"Good thinking there Josh," Sebastian said as we walked down the stairs. "Along with Cho's phone we might be able to get some good information. Assuming your friend can break into it."

"Oh, so it's not a company phone after all?"

"In a way it is. All Spyrius employees have standard phones that are centrally managed and properly secured. But I pay for the Oz employees to have a personal phone if they want. Kind of a perk. Randy usually kept his Spyrius phone at work but always had his personal phone on him. So yes, I paid for it, so I actually wasn't bending the truth there.

But since we don't manage it I am not sure if we will be able to get into it."

We went down to Dan's lab next to his office, where he was busy working on his laptop and Kyle was taking pictures of a cell phone with his cell phone.

"Hey guys, did you get interviewed?" Dan said in his friendly manner, and then added when he noticed us staring at Kyle, "He thinks Cho used a pattern for his phone, not a numeric password…"

"…So I'm taking a picture of it and then running it through this piece of software that enhances it allowing you to see the patterns left on the phone by skin oils," Kyle added interrupting Dan's chain of thought. "Sorry Dan," he added.

"Remember we're used to finishing each other sentences," I said.

"It's alright," Dan said laughing.

We filled them in on the interview and told them that they would not be needed, which everyone felt was good. Then Sebastian gave Randy's phone to Kyle.

"Here's another present for you. See if you can get into these phones and then get everything you can from them. Hopefully they will be able to tell us something about who else, singular or plural, Randy was working with. Dan can help you with anything you might need."

"We can also find out if Randy called Eusebio or vice-versa," Dan said. "I'm getting a place ready for Cho. It's not a pretty site, and I don't want to keep Oz locked out forever. Then I'll see how good Kyle is at forensically analyzing whatever's left of our log files. Give him a good test!"

I started thinking to myself this was all great for Kyle, and I know he was in heaven right now with school the last thing from his mind, but I personally needed to get back to school at some point.

"Umm, not to be an annoyance here, but at some point I, at least, need to get back to school. I really don't want to miss more than the first two days. We can't go through Oz as the projector is broken, and we are 3,000 miles away."

Kyle gave me a look that said 'why did you have to bring that up?'

"Don't worry about that right now," Sebastian said as he put his arm around me like I was some old friend. "I can get you back same day. Worst case we use my private jet. Don't worry about it right this second."

"So we are staying at least tonight?" Kyle asked all excited like a puppy waiting for a treat.

"Yes, of course. That's settled for now." Sebastian stated as if there would be no further discussion for the moment.

"Josh, can you come here for a moment?" Kyle asked motioning me to come to where he was.

I complied and Kyle whispered something quietly to me so the others would not hear. Normally I would have found what he said funny, but now I was suddenly annoyed at the mundaneness of the quest he asked me to carry out. But by that time I had given up.

"Is there a superstore around here? If we are going to stay the night we need to get a few things. Plus I'm hungry anyway."

"Great idea!" Sebastian said with an enthusiasm that surprised me. "Dan, Darlene's still here, right?"

"Yes, she's in her office."

"Great, Josh, grab Darlene and have her take you to the store and get what you need and come back with lunch for all of us."

So now I'm an errand boy, I thought. I just sighed and said okay.

I got a list of food wants from everyone and Sebastian gave me forty dollars to cover lunch. I grabbed Kyle's credit card to cover the other things as I didn't want my parents, who had access to my credit card online, to notice charges from Moses Lake, WA. Kyle's parents wouldn't notice, and wouldn't care if they did.

The drive with Darlene was very quiet as I don't think she wanted to talk about how she wanted Kyle to stay in front of me. Fortunately in a small town such as Moses Lake nothing is really too far from anything else so the drive was relatively short.

I realized that I had never bought underwear by myself in my life, and doing so felt strangely odd. My mom always did that. But here I was buying underwear not only for me but for Kyle which was stranger still (that's what he told me to get that he didn't want anyone else to hear). The point being that except for the shirts that Sebastian gave us I hadn't had a change of clothes since the morning before. I also bought a couple of shirts for us and, sox, and a couple of sweat pants for lounging around. The cargo pants I was wearing and the jeans Kyle had would have to last for another day. I did this while Darlene was looking at other things as it was embarrassing enough already.

The store had a sub shop inside of it where we picked up lunch for everyone. Dan wanted corned beef, his Irish roots showing through, but that would be too exotic for Moses Lake. So I got him a ham sandwich instead, his second choice. Sebastian may have spent time in California and seem like the typical high-tech Californian, but make no mistake he was from Texas and he ate meat. So a steak and cheese for him. I got a giant Italian sub that Kyle and I would split. Kyle was not very particular about his food so we saved a little by splitting a sub. Darlene got a turkey breast sub.

"So what do you think of our little town?" Darlene asked me heading back, obviously trying to make some sort of friendly conversation.

"It's fine I guess. My cousins live in a small town in upstate New York. Moses Lake reminds me of that, except that it doesn't have a lake running through the middle of town. But it's the same basic vibe."

"Yeah, the lake is great. During the summer there's all sorts of water activities: boating, jet skis, fishing, kayaking. Sebastian threw a couple of big parties on the lake for everyone at Spyrius this summer. He also takes people out on his boat. Last winter we did a big ski trip where he rented a bus, I think we're doing that again this winter..."

She went on about how much fun it was there, even talking a bit about Anya, Sebastian's model girlfriend who was with them on one of those excursions. For someone who was earlier saying how boring it could get she was making it sound exciting. She was just trying her best to make conversation, though it wasn't really conversation that interested me. I did find out that Sebastian was there probably only about sixty percent of the time and for the rest he was either back in L.A., visiting family in Texas or off someplace exotic with Anya.

We got back and the five of us all got together in a first floor conference room to eat lunch. By this time the police were gone and things seemed to settle back down into a normal work day. I did come to realize that it's not easy to eat a messy sub with one hand in a sling. Kyle had made significant progress on the phones and proceeded, with Dan's prompting, to update Darlene and me.

"So Cho's phone was a simple pattern and it didn't take me long to figure that out. Randy's was a bit more interesting, just got it finished before you came back. He had a password on it, and I have no idea what it was, but you can go on the phone carrier's website and ask for a new password. Now to do that you have to answer three password reset questions that Randy put in earlier. But those questions are so inane I just had to find three that Sebastian knew the answers to. For example, since they were in the same class he obviously knew the name of their high school class mascot: Smurfs. I think that's pretty funny."

"I didn't come up with it so don't blame me," Sebastian chimed in.

"So it then sends a new password to your alternate e-mail address. Guess what his alternate e-mail address is?"

Since Kyle seemed pretty excited it was obvious he was successful so I guessed a logical e-mail that he could get access to. "His Spyrius e-mail."

"Bingo! We got one of the Spyrius' e-mail admins, with Sebastian's approval, to grant us access to it. Once we got that we could get into the phone carrier's website under Randy's account. That's all we really need as we can get his personal e-mail from there, but we can also reset the device password, which I did, so now we are in that too."

"Very good, I'm proud of you," I said. "Did you find anything interesting?"

"Come on, you know that actually wasn't really very hard. Not like when we hacked the cell phone within your mom's car, spoofed it and sent fake messages to the SIM, then starting the car. Now that was real hacking."

"Yes, I remember. My mom was not too happy that it was possible to do that. But the phones?"

"Don't know yet, just finished getting in. Come down when we finish. You can help me go through them."

Normally I love working with Kyle on this sort of stuff, but I wasn't really into it today. But I had nothing better to do so I agreed. Dan said he had the room all ready for Cho and needed Sebastian's help to move Cho into the room that he created right next to his body. Then he would move the room to outside Oz proper just like what happened with the room Kyle and I were stuck in. After we all finished eating we all went back downstairs. Dan and Sebastian went off to one of the portal rooms while Darlene tagged along with Kyle and me, mostly to see what Kyle would find I am sure.

Back in Dan's lab, Darlene set me up with a laptop to use in case I needed it while Kyle started going through Cho's phone.

"There's a bunch of 509-334 numbers. Those are all Spyrius, right Darlene?"

"Yes, all our numbers start with 334. The area code of Moses Lake, and for that matter all of Eastern Washington, is 509."

"The only other number is 510-606-0842. And boy are there some interesting texts from this number. Josh, see what you can find on the number."

I did some basic Googling and reverse number lookups while Kyle read some of the texts. Fortunately, even with the sling, I could still use my right hand for typing.

"*Upload masking program, should work w/antenna. - Jai.*
That's from Saturday. Ah bingo. Here's from Cho to this person Sunday.
Need to set a trap as we talked about earlier. Have 2 rogues.
Right after from him
It works, like I showed u. Pick entry, in storeroom, can move. - Jai.
That's all at 8:15 yesterday morning. That's right after Randy found us and we escaped at Harvey Mudd."

"It's Oakland, California," I said after getting all the information I could get. The area code is Oakland, but there is no reverse lookup. It's not a land line, not that I expected it would be."

"That's all the texts from that number. There's a couple to Spyrius numbers, but they're very mundane, like
When u getting in tomorrow?"

"He wasn't supposed to be using his personal phone for actual Spyrius work, that's what the Spyrius phone is for. But those of us working on Oz aren't supposed to mention Oz in texts on any phone." Darlene pointed out.

"Well someone from Oakland, California was obviously working with Randy and Cho," I said stating the obvious. "Darlene I assume a Jai from Oakland doesn't ring any bells?"

"Nope. Not at all."

"Let's see what what's in Randy's phone and e-mail. Josh, take his phone, I can check his e-mail on the laptop."

I took his phone and looked through his call and text history. There was not a single text so he either never texted, or cleared his texts often. What was there was his call history, and interestingly was that a call from a 509 area code at 7:15 pm yesterday. I looked up the 335 exchange and sure enough it was Pullman. WSU to be exact. I also noticed that 510-606-0842 number, a few over the last few days. There were a bunch of other numbers that might be interesting. The history only went back a week, probably the last time he cleared it.

"Jaivana1720, that's the Jai. There's some e-mails to and from that person, but we got a problem."

"What?" Darlene asked Kyle.

"They're using PGP encryption for their e-mail. They are all encrypted, I would need the passcode. And I will bet Randy's not using 'password1234' as his passcode."

"Can it be broken?" Darlene inquired.

"Theoretically. I have heard that NSA can break PGP, but I doubt I will be able to, at least not right now and not without a lot of help."

"What about brute force?" she asked.

"Possible. We can try to brute force the private key passphrase. It could work. That could take anywhere from minutes to days, and no guarantee of it working at all. But that doesn't help us right now. Seems Randy was a little more security conscious then Cho."

"It's a cannon," I said.

Both Kyle and Darlene looked at me quizzically so I elaborated, "Jaivana is a large ancient cannon from India cast in, get this, 1720. That's our hacker's handle."

"Hmm," Kyle said in thought. "Let's just assume this guy is a self-aggrandized jerk, so he probably has a name that reflects on him somehow. I'll bet he's from India, or maybe his name has something to do with cannons or both."

"That really narrows it down."

"It might. We know he's from Oakland, so that narrows it some."

By now we had noticed that Dan and Sebastian had returned to Dan's office and we overheard them talking about finishing up the process of moving Cho's body and reopening Oz.

"I think the most important thing is obviously that this Jaivana guy was sending stuff to Cho based on Oz code," Kyle said. "So he may have a hidden virtual private network into Oz and that would be the most important thing to find. We'll need Dan's help on that. Let's catch them up on where we are."

"And I found out Eusebio called Randy, not the other way around. Bet Sebastian will be very interested in that."

Chapter 20

We walked into Dan's office. Cho's body had been put into a below freezing, climate controlled coffin and moved right outside Oz proper. The best that could be done for the moment. We caught the two of them up on everything we had done.

"We still don't know if Eusebio was actually in on Randy's plan or if he was just asked by Randy to call if anything unusual happened," said Sebastian. "But I can take care of that, I agree the most important thing is to see if that hacker Randy was working with has some way in."

"I can shut off any outside access for now," Dan said. "It's going to be a pain trying to find where a rogue VPN could have been inserted."

"I thought you kept snapshots of the code so you could compare changes?" Darlene asked. "That's how you found the room Kyle and Josh were in."

"Yes, but I only do a comparison if I actually suspect something. Who knows how long ago that was set up, and the code had changed all over the place since then probably."

"If only we had a record of the network traffic in and out of here." Kyle mused.

"Oh yeah, I do have SpyriusShark logs archived," Dan remembered. "I log all traffic outside of the Intranet. Good point: that would be the only persistent connection outside the ones we know of."

"The actual traffic will probably be encrypted, but we should be able to find it and then that will help us search for the connection in the code and shut it down," Kyle added.

"Well you two work on that," Sebastian directed. "Josh and Darlene, why don't you two take up looking at the rest of Randy's e-mail and see what else we might be able to procure from it. I'm going upstairs to have a little chat with Eusebio."

Darlene and I worked well together since, unlike during the car ride, we actually had something to focus on. Between the e-mail and his phone we identified two groups of people Randy intended to sell the Oz technology to. One of these groups was most likely the two men in suits we saw at the Town Square. These e-mails were unencrypted, probably because it's too hard to set up the encryption unless you really know what you're doing, but they were definitely talking in code. But we did ascertain the foreign country they came from. Good information to pass along to Sebastian.

Kyle and Dan did exactly what they set out to do. They found the rogue IP addresses in the SpyriusShark sniffer logs. Ironically when Kyle asked me to check on the IP, it was from Oakland. The guy was so self-assured he didn't even try to hide his origination point by running through a proxy like we did with at Sylvia's house.

"He's probably so narcissistic he doesn't think anyone will find him, so he doesn't try to hide himself too much," Kyle noted.

"Why do you assume it's a he?" Darlene asked a little miffed at the gender assumption.

"Just playing the odds, that's all. Sorry, I'll use gender neutral pronouns if you like."

I wasn't quite sure if Kyle thought Darlene was really upset, I don't think she was, but she dropped the conversation and they went back to work. By this time Sebastian had returned.

"Talked to Eusebio. Obviously he has heard about the shooting by now. He claims that he knew nothing about Randy's intentions to sell the Oz technology. Randy asked him to let him know if anything odd happened, but to keep mum because Randy wanted whatever he was doing to be a surprise. I tend to believe him, but I can't fully trust him. Most of his work was done anyway and he understood the parting of ways. Oh, and I think he has no idea about the shooting that happened in his bedroom."

"What's to stop him from telling other people about Oz?" I asked.

"Well nothing can truly stop him, but anyone who joins this program signs a very nice legal document stating you will never discuss the Oz program with anyone. Mostly I doubt anyone will believe him. Without proof, very few people would really believe it. That said, I agree it's going to get harder and harder to keep it a secret. Josh got me thinking when we were talking about it yesterday. I need to start planning how to publically announce this so that if I am forced to at some point it will be done right."

Dan and Kyle continued their work, and having found the address they were able to find the code where the tunnel was set up.

"Pretty ballsy," Dan remarked. "They literally buried the code for the tunnel inside the main code, and in such a way that when others modified Oz using the specialized high-level language I created, it would not overwrite their code when the new base code was written. Too bad this guy, or girl," he said that with a smile toward Darlene, "is a bad apple, otherwise he would be a good addition."

"How did he get the code in there in the first place?" I asked.

"I'll assume that Randy actually shipped him the raw code, for which this hacker put in his code and sent back to Randy, who then overwrote my code. Since I had no reason to suspect anything I never checked to see if my code was modified. Did I not tell you Sebastian that Randy had no need to have rights to my code?"

"Yes, you did, and yes, you were right, but I just went with Randy's insistence that in order to have the best security he needs to know and have access to everything. Obviously I made a mistake there," he said with a smile. "Nothing I can do now but learn from it."

"So I assume you are going to delete that tunnel..."

"...Already have," Dan quickly interrupted me, "and added code to alert me if any new tunnels are set, just in case."

"Won't this person still have all the code for Oz?"

"That's a good point Darlene," Dan said. First, he doesn't have the specialized hardware to run it. To be honest to someone who just had the code it would look more like a first person shooter video game. There is nothing in the code to portend that this is truly a virtual world you can enter. Second, let's just say I have some additional protections that I'm not going to comment on."

"Like what, some sort of logic bomb that will erase the code or something?" Kyle asked.

I think Kyle was close as Dan did seem a bit taken aback. He said nothing, so Kyle pressed.

"Well if that was the case and he saw the code delete itself the first time then you would think when he downloaded it again he would find the bomb and disarm it?"

Dan thought for a second. "Well Mr. Smarty Pants, let's just assume you might be in the right area. What other things might I have done to protect the program from such a scenario? That will be your homework assignment for tonight."

"So the VPN is deleted and he can't get back in. There's no Randy to let him back in," Sebastian said, "I think we should make an effort to find who this guy is at some point, but for right now I guess that ends it. He can't really do anything without exposing himself, and the code itself it pretty worthless without all the hardware and infrastructure behind it."

"What about the people who were trying to buy the whole thing? What are you going to do about them?" Darlene asked.

"What can I do? What can they do? I don't think there is anything anyone is going to do. Same with Bradley, I don't think he really *can* tell anyone about this. No, I think this whole adventure with Randy trying to sell Oz, and Josh and friends finding Oz, and multiple shootings happening is finally over. At least for now."

"So that's it?" Darlene asked like something was missing. "This whole adventure we've just been through and the final scene just plays out like that? We shut down his, or her, access and that's it? Seems like there should be more."

"A bit anti-climactic," I said.

"Would make for a pretty lame ending if this was a movie," Dan added.

"I know, you would think the climax of this whole adventure would be a bit more monumental," Kyle said, as he stood up and started acting out the final scene. "The hacker Jaivana, is cornered in a dark alley by our heroes," he narrated. "That's us, we're the heroes" he said breaking form before going back. "The trapped antagonist shoots, injuring one of our heroes before he ducks into an old abandoned warehouse. Our heroes follow through the catwalks of the dark warehouse. Shots ring out from both sides, glancing off steel pipes."

By this time he was on a roll, animating everything, flailing his arms about. He continued.

"The villain lures one of our heroes into a dead-end trap. He has him dead to rights and fires. A sure death. But his gun his empty. They fight, hand-to-hand, each almost falling to the depths below. Just as it all looks hopeless and our hero is hanging from one finger, one of the other heroes throws an iron pipe like a spear, hitting Jaivana, knocking him off balance and he falls over the catwalk tumbling down. Landing in a vat of acid, he screams as he slowly retreats into the bubbling liquid. The end."

We all stood there in awe of Kyle's impromptu performance. Darlene clapped.

"Um, I think I've had enough shooting and excitement for now," Sebastian finally said. "I don't mind a nice quiet resolution."

"But I liked the story," Dan added.

"Would make for a better movie," I said.

"But I didn't even get to the part where we wipe out the foreign spies…" Kyle trailed off.

"You know, it's funny in a way," Darlene added. "Neither side can really do anything. Kind of like a Mexican Standoff."

"Not really," Kyle said back to his normal self. "A true Mexican Standoff is with three people, not two."

Everyone looked at Kyle assuming they were going to get further explanation. Kyle obliged.

"Our situation is with two parties. And it's not a true standoff at all since we are both standing down. Neither of us has a loaded gun pointed at the other so to speak. You see in a duel, with two people, you have the incentive to shoot first, as obviously the person who shoots first has the advantage of being able to kill the other person before that person kills him. But in a Mexican Standoff, with three people in a triangle, no one wants to shoot first. If Person A shoots Person B, then Person C will shoot Person A and win the standoff as the other two will be dead. So there is no incentive for any of the three to shoot first, hence the standoff. It was the final scene of some famous Western movie from the Sixties, but I can't remember the name."

Dan, Darlene and Sebastian all stared at Kyle after he finished his in-depth and detailed description.

"Is he always like that?" Dan asked me.

"After five years now I've gotten used to it," I said with a laugh.

All of a sudden I could see the look of fear in Kyle. It's a look I've seen many times before when he suddenly realized that he has overstepped the bounds of societal norms. He had acted like a frenzied movie director and then suddenly a condescending know-it-all. He was starting to feel comfortable around these people, letting his guard down and acting like his true self. Suddenly he realized that might have been a mistake and I knew he suddenly felt he blew it. But I could tell from all three of them that they were taking it in stride.

"Kyle, it's okay. Dan didn't mean anything negative," I said hoping Dan would pick up on what I was seeing, and he did.

"Kyle, don't worry. I just thought it was amusing that you were all animated describing the final scene in our adventure one moment and then meticulously describing the finer points of a Mexican Standoff in exquisite detail the next. Remember Kyle, everyone on the Oz project, and almost everyone that works for Spyrius as a whole are smart and geeky. So you fit in just fine, even if you can be a bit of a smart-aleck."

He said the last part with a wry smile. I could see the relief from Kyle.

"Gee, Dan. It almost sounds like you are offering Kyle a job here," Darlene stated.

"Well, umm, you see, Sebastian has final say, you know. But I would recommend Kyle for a position at Spyrius working on the Oz project. Along with the fact that I am sure he can program fine, I think his forensics and hacking skills are sorely needed. Sebastian?"

"Hmm," he mused while rubbing his chin. "Well, you do have the pedigree from your father, and Darlene would probably like having someone else her age around. Yes, Kyle, I think, with Dan's recommendation, I would like to offer you a job with Spyrius Technology working on the Oz project. The position will be full-time with all normal benefits." Then he added, "If you accept, of course."

I could see the wild-eyed excitement in Kyle's face. This was his dream job and dream company. Then he looked at me and froze. Oh, I knew there was no way he would turn down the job, but I knew he just had no idea how to accept without feeling like he was somehow betraying me. Of course the idea of my best friend suddenly being 3,000 miles away caused a twinge in my heart. There was also a little jealously on my part. After all the excitement we had been through the thought of going back to the boring normalcy of college while Kyle would get to work here did make me a bit envious. But I had to be bigger than that, so even though I should have probably made Kyle stand up on his own and accept, I fell into the old habit of just answering for him in these situations.

"Of course Kyle is going to accept your offer," I said to Sebastian. Then I turned to Kyle, "You are going to accept this job offer, right." I said that more as a command then a question.

"I guess," he said with a little hint of tears starting to well up in his eyes. Tears of joy, of course. He smiled a bit smile and mouthed a little thanks to me.

"That's set then. Kyle, you are now a Spyrius Technology employee," Sebastian stated. "We'll have all the paperwork for you tomorrow morning after Human Resources does its thing. Josh, upstairs to my office with me right now."

I'm not sure why Sebastian was ordering me to his office. I supposed I could have refused, but I'll give Sebastian the fact that he did have a certain charisma that made you want to follow him. So I did.

"The movie is, *The Good, the Bad and the Ugly* by the way." Sebastian said with smile as we walked away. "See, Kyle, we all can be a bit of a know-it-all!"

Chapter 21

Upstairs in his office he sat behind his desk and pointed me to a chair. I sat down. My legs still hurt though they were doing better.

"Tell me Josh, what do you think of the Oz project?"

I wasn't really sure what he was looking for, so I answered it pretty straight. "It's amazing. Not much more to say. I mean, it's probably one of the greatest technological breakthroughs that I will witness in my life. And it's just plain cool. Did you just want me to stroke your ego?"

"No. Actually I am looking for the opposite. Tell me, Josh, I assume you think your friend will make a good addition to our team here?"

Once again I had no idea what he was trying to get at so finally I got the nerve to ask him.

"Yes I do, but why do you keep asking me about Kyle and my opinion on things, putting me up at the whiteboard to lead a conversation, sending me out to get lunch, etcetera? What are you getting at?"

"Look, Josh, I think Kyle is going to be a great employee, he's incredibly smart, has great computer skills, but I need more than just people with great technical skills. This company is growing and the Oz project is growing. I need people with common sense and the ability to think on their own and figure things out and trustworthiness. I think you fit that bill."

He paused to let that sink in.

"You want to offer *me* a job here? Why?"

"Why? Why not? Do you not think you could be an asset here? Do you not think the Oz project would be an amazing thing to work on?"

"Of course this would be an amazing thing to work on. But I'm not a genius like Kyle. He can run rings around me in programming, hacking, hardware and pretty much anything related to computers and technology."

"Yes, but I need more than just people with excellent technical skills. I need people who can help figure things out about Oz, what we can do with it, what it can be used for. I'm not saying you're the greatest visionary in the world, but from what I have seen you can lead, figure things out and use common sense; I need those things. You've taken everything I have thrown at you in stride, even when I put you in uncomfortable situations. You are obviously willing to take risks. May I remind you that you turned down ten thousand dollars cash to move apartments because you were skeptical about why someone would make such an offer. How many college students would do that? Even though you are so young, I don't think you are afraid to tell me when I am wrong or disagree with me. Actually the fact that you are so young is an asset in itself as I need some youthful, original ideas."

I really didn't know what to say. I was a bit dumbfounded. I had actually almost forgotten about the ten grand we turned down.

"Look, Josh, my father was a very smart man and he made a lot of money in the oil business, but it was all old school politics with people scratching each other's backs, people sucking up to those in power. My dad had more 'yes men' than he knew what to do with. When I started Spyrius Technologies and the Oz project I vowed I would run it the opposite way. I want people who bring in fresh ideas, have a passion for what we are doing and who will challenge me. So far we have done some amazing things with Oz, but it's only just a toddler taking its first steps. There is so much more to explore with this technology."

"And you think I could be a contributor to this?"

"Only if you think you can, and if you think you have the passion for it. Randy notwithstanding, so far I have been a damn good judge of character. Look at Dan. We were rivals in school. I have a blue blood Texas oil background; he's from Irish immigrants who scraped out a living. He went to Harvey Mudd based on talent alone, not what his family name was. We have nothing in common and yet I knew he would be perfect for this, and he has been. Look at Darlene. She's only seventeen and heck, I almost fired her dad when I found out she was helping design the Oz Creator program. But then I realized how much enthusiasm she has even though she's only a passable programmer, don't ever tell her I said that, so I hired her and she has worked out great."

I really was taken aback. Maybe I was better than I thought I was. Maybe I was selling myself short and he saw something in me I was unsure of. Or maybe he had other motivations.

"First I want to make sure of some things. Are you trying to hire me just to appease Kyle because you think he will work better if I am around? Because if so I think that's totally off. In fact, to be honest, even though I may not like it, I think Kyle might do better if I wasn't around because that will force him to have to do things on his own instead of just relying on me."

"Bingo. That's what I mean. First, I couldn't agree more, and I think that is an issue that will need to be addressed. But look, you evaluated the situation and expressed the honest solution, even though it doesn't benefit you. I want that; I need that. So then you tell me, what would you do so Kyle can blossom but yet still have you around as a friend?"

"Well I guess I can start by not answering things for him like I did back there. By encouraging him do more things on his own without my input, even if he fails. Oh, but how am I going to make him aware of that?"

"Just tell him. I find that works wonders. I don't think the problem is you and him being best friends or getting a place together. Just let him be and be supportive. Yes, he's a little quirky, but this is a very safe environment for him. I think you will find he will fit in better than you think."

"Okay then. Number two: I know about Oz. Not only Oz, but other than Dan, Darlene, Kyle and you I am the only one who knows about what happened in Pullman. There are plenty of other people out there who are as smart and have as much common sense as me. Are you sure you don't just want to keep me close by so you can keep tabs on me?"

"Very astute of you, Josh. If you want to know the truth that is a nice side effect of hiring you. But Josh, this world has billions of people. Of course there are others who have the same qualities I'm looking for. The point is, sometimes life is a bit of luck. You did happen to stumble on Oz, and you do already know just about everything, so now I don't have to risk telling someone new about it. But no, to answer your question. If I didn't think you would excel here I wouldn't offer you a job. There may be others who could also excel here, but I think you could, too. And I think you will."

"And what if I don't work out? I mean, you are asking me to leave college for this."

"No one knows what's going to happen in life. I'm offering you a position because I think you will succeed and thrive here. Now it's up to you to decide if you think you will. Oh and one last thing, you did help save this company and probably my life as well. And no, that is not part of why I am offering you a job, so don't even ask. But, for the record, I am grateful."

He said that last part with a smile. Maybe he wasn't so bad after all.

"Go down, get Kyle and bring him up. I need to discuss a few things with both of you, that is, if you're taking the job. You can use the elevator ride to make up your mind."

He was smiling again. Basically giving me a few minutes to decide. I went out to the elevator lobby and pressed the down button. Yeah, I had already decided. No matter what the reasons, how could I possibly turn down the opportunity? No regrets, they say. The elevator came. I took the special access badge that's used to access the basement housing Oz, slid it in the card reader and went down to get Kyle.

Kyle was still in Dan's office when I told him Sebastian wanted to see him. We walked out of Dan's office together.

"Josh, let's take the stairs up. There's something I want to talk to you about."

"Okay," I said interested in what he had to say first. We went to the seclusion of the stairway.

"This isn't fair," he said. "I don't know if I can do this without you. Maybe if we asked Sebastian we can get you a job at Spyrius proper. I'm sure there is some position that he can put you in and then you can rise up and maybe work on the Oz project eventually."

"Oh, so you don't think I'm good enough to work on the Oz project now?" I was going to have a little fun with this.

"No. Come on, I don't mean that. If I had the choice we would both be hired for Oz. But you know me, I'm not all good in situations where I'm not comfortable and don't really know anyone. Having you around will make it much easier. Plus you're my best friend. Are you just fine with us suddenly being thousands of miles away from each other?"

"Kyle, maybe it's the best thing for you. Maybe you need to figure things out on your own without me around. Maybe I've coddled you too much and haven't forced you to confront your social anxiety. Maybe what you need is for me not to be around."

I said that pretty strongly and he just looked at me with stunned silence. Yes I was having a little fun with this, but Sebastian was right. If I was going to stay I did need to change how I interacted with Kyle. He needed to become more socially independent. We walked up to the first floor, took the elevator to the top, went into Sebastian office and sat down.

"Well?" he asked looking at me.

"I'm in."

"Good. I'll have Human Resources draw up all the papers for you. Then we will get the two of you back home to get all your stuff, back here and I expect you to start first thing Tuesday morning after the Labor Day holiday. We'll have badges, laptops and places for you to sit by then."

Kyle looked very confused.

"You didn't tell him," Sebastian stated.

"Nope. So, Kyle, I have accepted a job working at Spyrius on the Oz project. I hope you don't mind."

His eyes looked like two daggers aimed straight at my heart. He was seething and about to say something, but I cut him off.

"Look, I am serious about what I said back there. I haven't been fair to you. You need to get out on your own more." And then just as an afterthought I added with a smile, "Maybe Darlene can help with that some."

He just sat there, blushing a little. I don't think he knew what to say.

"Two things. First your salary," Sebastian said as he handed each of us a piece of paper with a number on it. I looked at mine and was in shock. It was a large number, at least to a broke eighteen-year-old college kid. I looked at Kyle. He seemed to be in shock, too. He looked a little concerned and I think he was worried that his number was bigger than mine. I assumed Sebastian figured we would tell each other our salaries so I showed Kyle my number. It was the same as his, and he seemed relieved.

"It's just a starting salary. There's room for growth. Of course, you will get all normal benefits: health insurance, profit sharing, 401K and whatever else we offer that I can't think of off the top of my head."

If that was the starting salary... I thought to myself.

"Second you need to sign these."

He handed us each two four-page documents. One for Spyrius proper and one for 'additional projects', which was code for the Oz project. They basically stated that we would not discuss anything related to Spyrius or the 'additional projects' with anyone outside. We agreed not text, e-mail, blog, talk to the press or anything else under penalty of losing our first-born. It didn't really say that, but it did promise strict financial penalties, immediate termination and other nasty things. I wasn't sure how enforceable some of those really were but it got the point across.

"A bit harsh," I said.

Sebastian just smiled. What was I to do? Kyle had already signed his and gave it back. I was going to tell him that he should at least read it first, but I stopped myself. I needed to let him make his own decisions. I read mine before signing it and giving it to Sebastian.

"Oh, and one last thing. Here, one for each of you. The latest high fashion."

That he said with a little sarcasm as he handed us each a bright-red collared Spyrius knit shirt.

"Don't worry, you don't have to wear them. Now go down and hang out with Dan and Darlene for a bit. Give me a half hour and then we will head back to my place and call it a day."

Dan was thrilled to have me aboard. Darlene initially seemed to have mixed feelings. I think she liked the fact of having a third person her age working at Spyrius, but on the other hand I think she thought I might put a little chink into whatever long-term plans she had for Kyle. She considered it for a second, but then she smiled and gave me a big hug. I guess she figured the good outweighed the bad.

"This calls for a celebration. Round of pints on me. Oh yeah, we can't do that. Okay, dinner on me then."

Sebastian didn't come along, which I think he did on purpose to let us bond together. It was a lighthearted affair. We mostly talked about the ins-and-outs of working at Spyrius, what there was to do in Moses Lake, the best places to eat and so on. Darlene did mention a movie she wanted to see and asked Kyle if he wanted to go next week. He got the hint, said yes and didn't invite me or anyone else. After we were done, Dan dropped us off at Sebastian's house.

Sebastian was busy, so Kyle and I basically spent the rest of the evening hanging out in his cavernous living room. Sebastian did come down for a little general conversation, but soon retreated back up to his master suite area. Barbara, the housekeeper, had already retired to her quarters off of the garage by this time leaving just Kyle and I.

"So, one thing, Josh."

"What Kyle?"

"Well, I don't want to make you mad, and I know what you said earlier about doing things on my own. By the way, notice I accepted Darlene's invitation all by myself and will go all by myself?"

"Yes, I'm so proud of you," I said chuckling.

"But we have to live somewhere. So are we getting a place together?"

I actually hadn't really thought about that. But after the whole episode this summer with the apartment and leaving Kyle out I thought it would be pretty hard to say no. Plus, to be honest I was also moving to a strange place far away from home. Having a familiar face around would make it easier on me too.

"With the combined money we're making and the inexpensive housing market here, we can afford a proper house to rent. So yes, we can get a place together, I don't think I'm worried about us killing each other anymore."

Epilogue

"Good to see you two. I can't believe you are going through with this," Sylvia said as she gave both Kyle and I big hugs.

Larry greeted us too, though rather soberly. Larry may be easy-going, but he is not one who likes change, especially sudden and not of his making. I don't think he was happy with my decision to pull out of school. They would have to find another roommate, which most likely meant living with a stranger. I know Larry wished we never got the wrong apartment in the first place. He and Sylvia seemed to be getting along after his little breakdown, or so Sylvia said. Still, there seemed to be some tension.

Let me back up a bit. Before moving to Moses Lake permanently, Kyle and I had to get our stuff. Then there was the issue of telling our parents that we had to get out of the way. We flew back on Wednesday. Yes, we did get to fly in Sebastian's private plane, but only as far as Seattle, then we boarded a regular domestic flight back to Washington D.C. Still, it was an amazing experience being in a private jet. It was pretty small, only seating six passengers, but still something I never thought I would experience. Darlene made it perfectly clear that she was not happy that we got to fly in it, as she had yet to have a chance.

Springing the news on my parents was not easy. I can understand how it must have looked from their point of view. A few days ago they had dropped their eighteen-year-old son off at Virginia Tech. A couple of days later he shows up at home saying he's just come from Moses Lake, Washington but can't quite say why or how he got there, and drops the bomb that he's leaving school to take a job with the mysterious Spyrius Technology. The arm in a sling being icing on the cake. Needless to say, they were not particularly happy and they were very, very puzzled. I think ultimately they realized that I was going to do this, regardless of what they said, and begrudgingly supported me. My mom had a lot of tears that I was moving so far away, but I promised to call often. Fortunately it was still early enough to pull out of classes and get a refund for school. I reassured them I could always go back if this didn't work out.

Kyle's dad wasn't even home, being off on some trip in Europe. When he did talk to him he was fine with it. Kyle said he actually sounded proud. His dad was a college dropout himself and did just fine so I think he figured Kyle would probably learn more at Spyrius then at Tech anyway.

My dad drove us down to Tech on Thursday to get our stuff. The plan was to pick up our things and then drive back that same day. It is four hours each way, but I spelled my dad driving for some of it. We stopped at Kyle's dorm first. He didn't have much stuff so that didn't take long. From there we went to the new apartment that Sylvia and Larry had moved into the day before. At one point we went back into the old apartment and replaced the projector lens that Larry had smashed with a new one Sebatian sent with us. We put the fixed projector back into the hiding place in the sixth floor room ready for that Evan guy to use.

"So, you're really going," Larry said as the four of us sat around the kitchen table. I asked my dad to go get some food and he got the hint that we wanted a little time just the four of us.

"Yeah, after all we have been through, it's an opportunity we can't turn down," I answered.

"If you didn't you would kick yourself forever," Sylvia added.

We had filled them in on some of what had happened. We told them about the shootout with Randy and why my arm was in a sling and my legs hurt a little, though they were getting much better. That was public knowledge anyway. We did leave out the whole side excursion to Pullman and what happened to Cho, as there was no need for them to know that and there were still some loose ends there.

"You do realize," I said to both Sylvia and Larry, "that you can't tell anyone what you did or saw in Oz, right?"

"Our lips are sealed, and I mean that," Sylvia promised.

"Do you think I want people to think I'm crazy?" Larry said. But then I think he realized that I was pretty serious. "Don't worry, Josh. Neither of us will say a thing to anyone about what happened. Personally I just as soon forget the whole ordeal ever occurred in the first place."

Sylvia and Larry were a loose end that worried Sebastian. He was especially paranoid after what happened with Randy, a person he thought to be one of his most trusted friends. But there was nothing else to do other than ask the two of them to promise not to say anything, and I was pretty confident that they would keep mum on everything.

We reminisced a bunch about the year before until my dad got back with pizza. After eating we had to go, we still had a long drive ahead of us.

"Keep in touch, I love you both," Sylvia said hugging both of us again.

"It's been real," Larry said as he shook both Kyle's and my hands.

And then we left.

We spent Friday and Saturday at home, the last days of normalcy with our respective families. On Sunday Kyle and I took off. We had a commercial flight to Spokane, WA, and then we had a rental car waiting for the hour and a half drive to Moses Lake. No private plane this time. Sebastian put us up in one of those extended stay hotels in town and gave us the rental car. We had a month to find a place of our own and get a car for the two of us, which would be plenty of time. He said he would give us advances for any deposits and for a cheap car, since obviously we had no money ourselves. Of course our parents would have helped us out, but we were doing this on our own now.

During the quiet moments on our drive down I reflected to myself about what Spyrius had unleashed. What had currently been realized with Oz was only the tip of the iceberg for possibilities with this new technology. I feared that Randy was not going to be the only or last person to try to use it for evil purposes and that the ordeal we just went through was only a precursor to what might happen in the future.

Mostly, though, we focused on the positive. Kyle and I talked about how excited we were working for Spyrius, working on Oz, the new town, getting a place together, and especially for Kyle, Darlene. As we pulled into town, with the big lake off to one side, we had no idea what the future would bring for us, but we were pretty sure it would be an adventure.

www.ingramcontent.com/pod-product-compliance
Lightning Source LLC
Chambersburg PA
CBHW021230130626
46554CB00004B/1418